CATNIP

MAY SAGE

Catnip

Age of Night book 3

May Sage © 2017

Cover by Rebecca Frank

Photography by Lindee Robinson

Edited by Lisa Bing, Theresa Schultz and Sue Currin

FLIGHT

They were all screwed.

Coveney's animal jumped out of the way, blocking the attack of the Vergas wolf with ease, and buried his sharp fangs in his flanks. A pained growl was ripped from his chest and he turned to see an arrow lodged in his shoulder.

Shit. His tiger wouldn't be able to get rid of it, and shifting back to his human form in the middle of this mess was nothing short of suicidal. He'd only taken a second to contemplate how utterly screwed he was when another wolf jumped him from the right; he saw another set of arrows flying at him on the left.

Arrows...

He knew someone who used those, and she rarely missed her mark.

You're so dead, he told himself. He was - there was a very good chance that they all were. But inside their home, there were nine children, at least two of whom would die if he failed, so he didn't have a choice. He needed to fight.

Zack, his Alphas' newborn son, was condemned by shifter laws because of what he was: a Turner, able to change a regular human being into one of them. Their existence was a secret that shifters had spilled a lot of blood to keep under wraps.

Lola, their toddler, wouldn't live much longer. There was a chance that the Vergas wolves had come because of Zack, too, but Coveney doubted it. They had wanted to kill Lola for a long time, hunting them everywhere, until his Pride had managed to push back.

But today, if things went their way, these wolves would have a chance, unless he stood his ground as long as possible to give the children a chance to run with their Beta female.

He had to survive.

Launching himself at the wolf, Coveney's tiger roared as a second arrow pierced his skin, closer to his heart this time.

It wasn't the first time he'd been shot. It hurt like a bitch, but he could ignore the pain. He had to.

His claws ripped through the wolf's back; he placed a paw on its head and, with a flick of his wrist, broke its neck. Then he turned left, facing the direction where all those damn arrows had come from, and there she was. Smirking. Of course she smirked. She was finally getting what she'd wanted for the best part of a decade.

*L*orren hadn't always been that way. Back in the day, she'd actually been a sweet kid; his very best friend. He couldn't even pinpoint when things had started to change, exactly, but he remembered when he'd realized there was no going back, not for them.

Coveney noticed that women had tits late for a shifter. They were animals, and most of them got horny shortly after hitting puberty and shifting for the first time, but he was nineteen when he found a girl that fascinated him more than a video game. Lorren disliked Holly on sight, but Coveney figured it was just because of the usual best friend versus girlfriend rivalry. However, one day, he'd been called to his Alpha's office and found himself accused of rape.

Him. He'd been too shocked to utter a single word.

Oh, he'd fucked, wildly, savagely, but Holly had been

3

an eager participant, and she'd loved every second of it.

"I don't understand," he'd said. "Holly..."

But it hadn't been Holly who'd gone to the Alpha with poisonous lies. It had been Lorren.

With some distance, he now saw he'd been a dumb fool. Lorren had been into him; she'd probably seen them as a thing because there had been no other women in his life. Not that it justified the way she'd ruined his life, but, if he'd realized what had been going on, he would have acted differently. He might even have given things a try with Lorren, for the sake of their friendship; he liked his girlfriend well enough, but they both knew their relationship was casual. Shifters didn't complicate sex.

Instead, he'd been completely blind, and the betrayal had hit him even harder for it.

Almost everyone turned from him, believing her word over his. Holly, his family, his friends. There were a few notable exceptions. The Prince who left his family Pride, going with Coveney rather than letting him become a loner. Others followed, standing firmly between him and the mob. They'd become the Wyvern Pride in the following months.

They were everything to him. No wonder Lorren

smirked as everything he held dear was burning to the ground.

Lorren hated him more than ever since he'd been acquitted, no doubt. She got entangled in another lie, years after his departure, and the Royal Pride ordered a witch to cast a truth spell this time. His name was cleared in the process, when the witch saw fit to ask about what had happened back then. Coveney still felt bittersweet about the whole thing; sure, now everyone knew he wasn't the piece of shit they'd believed him to be, but at the same time, they hadn't believed him enough to get her tested back then. A simple spell and he might never have had to leave his home, his family.

Her punishment was becoming a Squire, a slave of the Royal Pride, which explained what she was doing here. If the Royal Pride had been called to fight against them, she'd be part of the attacking force.

Coveney saw a dozen familiar faces behind her. He was relieved to see his own family, and their Alphas, were notably absent. It would have been messed up if their King had come to kill his own grandson. But it looked like the Royal Pride hadn't sent anyone official after them - these were just a bunch of stuck-up idiots who'd acted on their own.

He could see Lorren's glee from a distance as she shot arrow after arrow - all in his direction. He had to deflect the adversary in front of him in a one on one *and* avoid getting shot again.

Coveney's tiger screamed out as a wolf head-butted him right in the shoulder where he'd been shot. Falling to his flank at the impact, he saw another arrow fly, aiming right at his heart now that he was knocked over.

He almost closed his eyes, but he was no coward, so he watched death coming at him.

A split second before the weapon found its mark, a high-pitched scream resounded in the skies.

Great. Eagles. The servants of the shifter council had joined the party. Not only was he going to die - he was dying knowing his Pride was doomed.

That was his last thought when the magnificent bird of prey descended, plunging at high speed towards the driveway-cum-battlefield.

And it caught the arrow in its talons, before batting its large wings and flying back up.

What the...

An eagle had saved him?

His tiger sniffed tentatively and caught a faint scent he wasn't ever going to forget. Olives. Lavender.

And blood.

Shit.

The eagle - the female eagle, if his sense of smell didn't betray him - had been shot by Lorren. She may not be injured badly enough to die on the spot, but it didn't matter.

Coveney knew that, like everything else Lorren touched, her arrows were poisonous.

DUTY

*T*he majestic bird of prey had, as usual, done more than her share. At Ava's request, she'd leapt out of her skin and saved the day, grabbing the arrow aimed at the heart of the feline she'd observed from a distance for longer than she cared to admit. Then, after another arrow grazed her wing, she'd carried on flying, bravely, and not only long enough to get them away from the battle. She'd stayed in charge of their body, knowing how little Ava could tolerate pain.

Poor eagle. A powerful, deadly beast, stuck with a wimp of a human.

You did well, birdie. Let me take over now.

She knew she had to put her big girl panties on; she was still bleeding, for one, and despite all her skills, her eagle couldn't tie a bandage. Secondly, she needed to take over, because if she didn't grow a spine, her eagle would start resenting her, some day. She might even stop listening to her at all- which was how shifters became feral.

The bird flew further into the woods, where they'd left her clothes and her car before setting out to meet the Wyvern Pride that morning.

Every day, Ava woke up, took a shower, brushed her teeth, and told herself in the mirror, "I'm going to go speak to the Wyvern Alphas today." And, every day, after lurking at the edge of their land, staying far away from their patrollers, she came home without so much as exchanging a word with a Wyvern.

Well, almost every day. A couple of weeks back, she'd come across a large, powerful, and ruthless tigress from their pride. Yeah, that had helped with the jitters. Strangely, she'd gotten away without losing any limbs.

And today...

She'd felt the change in the air as soon as she left her hotel room, and every single piece of her had been tempted to run. But she hadn't. Thinking of all the children they had playing around the pride house, thinking about the felines she'd observed from a distance for weeks, and, above all, thinking about that stern, stoic white tiger she hadn't failed to notice, she'd let her braver self take over, and flown at high speed around the entire territory to see what they faced. It wasn't often that Ava Flavia Dale could be proud of herself.

Shifting back, Ava cried out in pain, her hands pressing her side. The wound wasn't huge, so it shouldn't have felt like someone had plunged a white-hot knife inside her. Even she wasn't *that* much of a wimp. Swallowing her bile, she peeked at the wound, long enough to see some disgusting green discharge coming out. She sniffed and cursed out loud. Shit. Poison.

What was she supposed to do now?

Ava was particularly unprepared for the shitty cards life had dealt her these last six months. She'd been pampered. As the fourth child, the child no one really needed, her place in her flock had been embarrassingly privileged. She had the benefit of being treated and respected as a Dale, yet no responsibility fell on her shoulders. So, she'd spent her time helping her siblings - her elder brother, in particular. Richard had started to take over for their parents, but he was so severe, the rest of the flock practically trembled when he entered a room. Having her by his side had mitigated their reaction. She was the soft Dale. The one people smiled at and offered cookies to.

And then, six months ago, her entire world had collapsed.

She'd been on the run the entire time since; twice, those who wished to kill her had come close. The old family friend she'd run to now laid in a shallow grave because he'd helped her.

She wasn't the fourth child anymore. She was more than likely the only Dale left alive, and not for long, unless she got that wound looked at.

Painfully, Ava managed to pull her jeans up her legs. Dismissing her bra, she grabbed her t-shirt, but lifting her arms was excruciating, so she just pulled her leather jacket on.

She wasn't far from her inn. She could make it.

And then what? Unless the owner was miraculously well-versed in the art of manufacturing antidotes, and willing to administer it to a shifter, she was still screwed. She couldn't go to a hospital; regular human doctors hardly knew how to deal with shifters, and, anyway, they would ask questions. Origins, address, name. She couldn't afford that sort of trail.

She had access to a fairly large pile of cash, though. Thank fuck for nameless, untraceable Swiss bank accounts, held by bankers who still remained faithful to her family. She could hire a witch.

Where would she find one, though?

One name came to mind. The name had been the answer to every question she'd asked herself for months, but each time she'd thought of it, she'd trembled.

In her travels, at the rare times she'd come across other shifters, they'd mentioned him. Everyone knew him, or knew of him, in any case. In this part of the world, he was known as a benevolent loner, someone people could turn to when they really needed help. She knew better.

If she wanted to live, she was going to have to seek out Knox, all the while knowing that there was a very real chance he would take one look at her and rip her throat out. Knox wasn't benevolent. He certainly wasn't a loner, either.

But he could end the madness that had ripped her family apart if he so wished. He could also probably put her in contact with someone who could heal her.

Again: if he so wished. He probably wouldn't.

"We have to go our separate ways," Richard had told her, ignoring how she frantically shook her head.

The blood of their parents still soaked her long skirt,

but while their betraying butchers were occupied, she managed to get away. Then, she'd seen two of her siblings, Aria and Rupert, take a knife through the heart. The monsters who'd turned on them had also raped them both, first, while Ava hid in the secret corridors between the walls of her home, like the coward she was.

She crawled to safety when the murderers dispersed, and, finally, after putting every single skill in her arsenal to good use, she got out. Richard had found her as soon as she'd left Dale and stepped into Rome.

She couldn't lose Richard after all that - she just couldn't.

"If we're together, we'll be ten times easier to spot. They'll go after me," he'd told her, only managing to make her cry harder. "You'll get a head start. Then, you can fly far, far away from here. Fly to another country if you can, I know your bird can do it."

"Never," she'd yelled.

"Three thousand years, Ava. That's how far back our family goes. We're the first of our kind - the first eagles. Do you know what may happen to every eagle on earth if none of us live?"

She did know.

"America. You fly to America, you hear me? They

say the First Wolf is in America, somewhere. You need to get to him and ask him to step in."

Her eyes bulged in her face.

"He can end this, you know he can."

"But he's a monster."

The original monster her grandmother told her tales about, the boogieman that would come and eat her if she was naughty. She wasn't a kid anymore, but she recalled the tales.

"Those are just stories, Sister. And if they aren't, it doesn't change anything. I'll be on the run for months, or years. They have everything they need to track me. You? There isn't even a picture of you online, and I burned your room before leaving. You're safe. Find him, and get him to help, or every single one of us dies."

If he'd just told her to save her skin, she would never have left his side, but he had known better. He'd given her a mission she couldn't refuse. So she hugged him hard, and shifted, before running for her life, remembering a lesson she'd been taught before she could write. Her blood didn't belong to her.

She had to find the First Wolf. In New York, she learned that Fenrir went by Knox, nowadays. In Boston, she was told he sometimes came out of his den for his *friends*. In New Orleans, there were whispers of him lending his hand to a pride of felines a few months back. So, slowly, she'd crept closer and closer to her goal.

Six months, she'd survived. She'd live another day, she swore, dragging her feet all the way to her room. She collapsed on her bed and succumbed to the darkness.

CHOICE

The fighting stopped just as suddenly and violently as it had started. One second, they were surrounded by so many enemies they had no hope of living through the day; the next, the few amongst their enemies left standing were begging for their lives.

The woman who came to save the day looked like a Sports Illustrated model. What she did belonged in the realm of the impossible; at a flick of her wrist, a humongous wave rose from the nearby lake and took shape, undulating to wrap itself against the attackers' throats. She smirked as they were dragged to the bottom of the lake.

He should have been happy. Instead, he felt sick to his stomach. That wasn't a fight as much as an execution. Whatever creature these things, these Scions, were, he didn't want to deal with them. Today, they'd been on his side, but who knew what they'd do tomorrow?

"You're alright?" Rye asked him, catching his expression, right after the madness was over.

They'd made a deal with the devil, and won. Hopefully, they wouldn't live to regret it too much.

The Scions weren't the only reason why he was so wound up, though. Nor was losing a friend - a longtime friend he'd loved like a sister. Tracy would be missed and remembered.

But Tracy didn't make him pace through the dining room, muttering to himself.

"I'm fine. Rain cleaned my wounds," he replied.

Thankfully, he'd had a witch on hand. He might not have managed otherwise, as he knew how to take care of Lorren's venom, but her silver, wolfsbane, and belladonna blend of poison acted fast on shifters.

"I wasn't talking about your wounds," Rye replied. "I haven't seen you so agitated in a long time."

Coveney closed his eyes.

"There was an eagle," he said, finally. "A female, I think. She saved my life today; got in the way of one of Lorren's arrows."

Rye lifted a brow. "We don't have eagle allies."

A lot of eagles were hired by the shifter council, and no Alpha of their kind made allies amongst other races. Their laws forbid it.

"*I know,*" he snapped.

This made absolutely no sense.

"It could be that girl," Daunte piped up. "You know? The one who came to warn us. She applied to be part of the pride, I remember her face. Then, Clari jumped her in the woods."

"Oops?" his mate winced guiltily.

"She never turned up after that."

Rye nodded, acknowledging every piece of information he'd just been given. Then, he came to the conclusion Coveney had anticipated. "Sounds pretty weird to me. I'm grateful she helped us, but if she's lurked around for weeks without reaching out, she could very well be a spy, for all we know. We'll send someone to track her, and interrogate her, when things calm down. Right now, I need every one of you in the pride house, making sure no enemy is lingering around us, waiting for a chance to strike."

Yeah, he should have kept his mouth shut.

Coveney considered explaining himself; there was no

one he trusted as much as Rye. But he found himself at loss for words, unsure of how he could formulate what he wanted to say. The girl was poisoned, sure, but it wasn't a Wyvern problem. Rye wouldn't care. Coveney shouldn't care.

Make him care, his tiger roared.

He stayed silent. He'd never asked a favor of his Alpha, and he wasn't going to start now. Not when he already owed him so damn much.

He paced some more, for all of three minutes, before his steps led him out of the dining room.

He hadn't even crossed the entry hall when the door opened behind him.

"Have you lost your goddamn mind?" Daunte half barked, half whispered, careful not to be overheard by anyone in the dining room.

Shit. Everyone had seemed occupied, and Coveney was hardly the life of the party; he hadn't believed his absence would be noticed immediately.

Coveney had anticipated Rye's order because he understood it. There *was* a good chance that there still were enemies at their door, away from their wards, but close enough to catch an opportunity to strike against them. For now, their enemies might have lost, but they still wanted the pride's kids' lives.

Their absolute priority had to be protecting the pride. Coveney knew that. As Head Enforcer, he was familiar with pride politics. He also didn't give a shit. He needed to go find the bird. He needed it more than he needed his next breath.

He'd changed drastically after the incident in the Royal Pride. Not only because he learned what it was like to find himself considered a criminal and watch those he trusted turn their backs on him. He changed because he also saw people, who didn't have one reason to, give up everything for him. There was no way he could ever repay Rye and the others for leaving their pride to be with him. That slate would never be wiped clean, however much he tried. But, from that moment onward, he decided that he'd always get even. If someone was doing him a favor, he returned it. And he owed the damn bird. Big time.

He might just be going overboard. There was a chance she was just fine. But if he was right, if she'd been hit...

The least he could do was find out.

"You can't go against Rye's *orders* right now. We've *just* been attacked, dammit."

He stared at Daunte. His guilt trip was working, but he wasn't going to let it show. He didn't want any member of the pride to worry; he just didn't care as much as he cared about finding the girl.

Finally, the Beta gave up on their little stare-off, with a sigh.

"If you're gonna be a fucker, at least attempt to be an intelligent one. We have a decent tracker with us, for once. Take her."

Oh, yeah. That might have been smart.

He looked back towards the closed doors; Ace had called a very small number of close friends to join them - some had made it, others hadn't. Vivicia, a loner based in LA, had arrived amongst the first. As well as being unwaveringly loyal, the female also happened to be a wolf shifter. Coveney wasn't bad at tracking, as far as felines went, but wolves were indubitably better equipped for that sort of job.

But that would mean asking a favor. The idea was always repulsive to him, but he could deal with it this time; he owed nothing to Vivicia. Yet.

"I'll send her your way. And I'll cover for you for *four hours*. If you don't check in by then, I'll find you, and kill you myself."

THE INN

*U*nlike some Wyverns, Coveney hadn't spent a lot of time outside of his pride territory. Others had freelance jobs online, or friends they wanted to see somewhere in the world. Some of them had even lived in the regular human world for a time; Tracy, for example, used to have book signings. Rye, Daunte, and Ian, who dabbled in venture capitalism, put on a suit and went to some meetings every now and then.

Coveney took the role of Head Enforcer when the pride was created nine years ago, and he'd never left his post since. He didn't take holidays. For some reason, Rye still insisted on counting the time off he was owed; he had over two years, last time he'd looked. He'd probably never use any of it. He was mildly curious about some places in the world. Okay, more than curious. Exotic locations fascinated him, hence why he secretly watched the Travel Channel whenever no one was around. But he owed the Wyvern, and the least he could do was protect them.

Leaving the pride for four hours this evening was quite possibly the closest thing he'd ever done to taking some time off, and even that was born of duty.

That meant he'd rarely dealt with any other kind of sups. He knew felines, he knew witches, like Niamh, and seers, like Hsu. The rest he'd read or heard about, but he couldn't boast of having any first-hand experience with them, hence why Vivicia was making him feel uncomfortable.

Were female wolves supposed to be that big? He'd fought plenty of lupine over the last few years, but he'd never stopped to wonder about their gender. Still, even compared to the enemies he recalled, she seemed pretty damn huge. The animal was the size of a goddamn bear. His tiger carefully ran one step behind, although he could certainly take her, speed-wise. And the snarling; was that really necessary? They were all friends here.

The female stopped running quite suddenly and her quick, yet painful, bone cracking process started; half a minute later, a naked woman crouched on the floor. A *pretty* naked woman. He would have to be blind to fail to notice Vivicia, with her dark, sensual eyes, and all her smooth skin; like most shifters, she was fit - the amount of exercise they needed to stay sane saw to that - but she also had a fair amount of curves. He'd been more than conscious of her in the past. Today, neither he nor his tiger cared, single-mindedly focused on finding their elusive savior. It had been over three hours since she may have been shot. The poison could very well have taken hold by now.

He also shifted, after negotiating with his frustrated tiger who didn't want to let go quite yet. But he couldn't speak with the female in their animal form, as she wasn't part of the pride. Stupid, weird, magic mojo rules he didn't understand.

"I can't help if I don't know what the hell I'm tracking, Robocop."

She'd taken to calling him that for some reason. He hadn't bothered asking why.

"I told you."

"Yeah, an eagle. There's at least fifty dead ones around us, though. My wolf smells eagle everywhere north of the house."

He shook his head.

"She came from the east, and headed west, towards the town."

"I need more. Sorry, but I don't have her scent,

anything that belongs to her, and I haven't seen many eagles in the past."

Coveney sighed. If the she-wolf had issues catching her, what chance did *he* have?

You have her scent.

"She smelled of olive and lavender," he muttered, running his hand through his hair, pissed he didn't have more.

If Daunte was right, they had her name, her phone number, and other crap like that - any applicant who wanted to join the pride needed to leave that. He could try to track her electronically - or get Ian to do so, anyway - but they were running out of time.

Vivicia frowned and put her hands on the floor, before shifting back. She sniffed left, then right, before dashing across the woods, heading towards the town, this time.

He ran after her, staying on his human form, because she was already slowing down. They always left a few clothes here and there for situations such as these; quickly pulling a pair of track pants on, he started to make his way through their small town.

The pride house was the first home anyone coming through the woods could see, and then there were a few homes, a school, a bank, a bar, their Alpha's bakery, some restaurants, all on the main road. Vivicia ran through it all, arousing the interest of a few humans. None of them freaked though, just raising a brow.

Anywhere else in the world, that would have been weird, but their Alpha female had created a small shifter haven in Lakesides, long before they'd come. As they hadn't done anything to ruin that over the last year they'd spent here, they were accepted. So far. If they'd heard the racket their battle had caused just earlier that day, they might have been a little less friendly. Thankfully, Rain had erected wards around the town before it had all started. As the enemies had witches of their own, her wards around their own house hadn't held out, but they hadn't been concerned about the town, so the regulars remained blissfully ignorant.

"Is that a new pride member?" someone asked him as he passed. "Can't be a dog, right?"

He carried on running, not stopping to answer, because Vivicia had slowed down, finally.

They'd made it to a small inn at the other end of town.

Shifting back, Vivicia pointed to the old building.

"There." She wrinkled her nose. "I'm allergic to lavender."

He lifted a brow. It wasn't usual for shifters to have allergies, food intolerances, or anything like that, but it happened, especially to half-breeds. Perhaps one of Vivicia's parents was a regular. He didn't ask. Prying wasn't in his nature.

Coveney walked into the lobby of the inn, and was greeted by a man in his mid-thirties. The place seemed clean, although the decor left a lot to be desired. Taking it all in at a glance, his tiger bared his teeth at the idea of the bird staying there. It wasn't too bad, but it was no place for a shifter. They needed space. They needed a territory to call their own.

"You have a woman staying here," he said, leaving it at that, because he didn't know any more about her.

He should have looked at her damn application.

The man shifted uncomfortably.

"Our guest's privacy..." he started.

Coveney placed both of his elbows on the counter and leaned forward.

Three, two, one...

"There's only one at the moment. Second floor, the first door on the right."

Vivicia chuckled as she walked right behind him.

"Regulars." He could practically hear her roll her eyes. "What was that girl thinking, though? He could have given her location to just about anyone."

Coveney's generally well-behaved tiger growled in warning. He'd already thought of that; spelling it out wasn't doing anyone any favors.

As they approached, his own sense of smell picked up the trail. His steps got faster and faster because, along with olive and lavender, he got blood, and something else, something that made him want to wretch.

Shit. He hadn't been wrong. She'd been hit, and poisoned, too.

The room the innkeeper directed him to wasn't even closed, let alone locked; the door was slightly ajar, as though someone had gotten out in a hurry. He leaped and pushed it, his mind coming up with a thousand different ways how he might have screwed up and arrived too late.

He stopped dead at the door, as he took in his eagle in her human shell. Someone might as well have punched him.

He didn't know why. He hadn't given much thought as to what she looked like. It didn't matter. He owed her a favor and that meant she wasn't going to die today. No other motivation had moved him.

Coveney was screwed ten different ways, because the woman was pretty much fucking dying, and his damn cock didn't fucking care; it stirred, twitching in his pants.

Her long, layered hair fell in soft waves around her, and her soft, plump mouth breathed shallow breaths that should have alarmed him, not made him want to touch it. She wasn't wearing much - just shorts, and an open jacket. It shouldn't have mattered, nudity was natural to shifters. But it fucking did. He couldn't stop staring at her damn breasts.

"You're not dying," he said simply, because she didn't have a fucking choice in the matter today.

Or ever.

STRANGER

*H*e was pretty. So pretty from up close. He had long, long lashes and dark eyes; wavy blond hair like an Adonis. He smelled like wood, Muscat, and sin.

How come she was seeing Coveney close enough for her to smell him now?

Please don't be dead. Please don't be dead. Please don't be...

"Arrrrg!" she yelled, waking up to her flesh burning her.

She definitely wasn't dead, because death wasn't supposed to hurt so much. Unless she'd been sent to purgatory.

"What the hell!"

"Don't move. I'm almost done."

Now that she was a little more conscious, she could see that he had some sort of balm in his hands and he was applying it to her wound.

Oh, good. She bit her lip and did her best to stop herself from crying out, letting him do what he could.

"It hurts like a bitch, I know," he told her. "Rain had to cover half a dozen of my wounds with this shit."

He was talking to her. Moving his lips and all. Which meant she was supposed to somehow make herself talk back.

She carried on staring like a lunatic.

"You're a contradiction, Ava."

"How do you know my name?" she croaked, her throat feeling like sandpaper.

"Ran through your application to join our pride. I talked about what you did yesterday with the rest of the pride; turns out, Daunte had already seen you, and he remembered you from the prospective members."

"Is that how you found me?"

She frowned, concerned about how easily he'd read through the trail of breadcrumbs she'd left. She'd only listed a burner phone on her application, and she'd paid for it with cash. But if he had done it, others might have, too.

She had to get rid of the phone. Her stomach twisted; her brother might know her number. She'd given it to her bank, just in case he contacted them, too.

"Nah. I had a wolf helping me track you down. Figured you might have needed an antidote."

Now that the pain had receded some, she felt his hands more acutely. They weren't soft; he had calluses and rough, dry skin.

"So, Ava-no-last-name, who supposedly wants to join our pride, yet never turned up for our trials. What's your deal? Just based on that information, Rye figured you may be a spy."

"Rye?" she asked. It wasn't the first unfamiliar name he threw her way, but she was trying to make sense of what came out of his pretty mouth now.

"Our Alpha. Anyway, spy potential. But then, you go and warn us enemies were coming *and* you saved my life a few minutes later. So, yeah, contradiction is all I got."

She shrugged. "I was there. Almost made it to the door, too. Then, I saw the giants you were interviewing and I doubled back," she partially lied.

To be honest, she hadn't needed to *join* their pride;

all she'd been after had been an audience with their Alphas.

But there had been a chance they might just have locked her up, and called her enemies. Staying away and observing them had made sense. After weeks of looking into their little peaceful world, though, she'd found herself wanting to see if there was a place for her there.

He smiled. "My Alpha picked you to come here in person. Despite the lack of last name. And the fact that you're five foot two. You should have come."

She winced as he tied a bandage around her. Finding herself half sitting up, and ever so close to him, she felt awkward enough to start babbling.

"So, you're a designated healer?"

He'd done everything the hard way, so it was clear he didn't have healing powers, but prides without healers had a member who volunteered for first aid. It rarely was an Enforcer, though, and from what she recalled of when she'd observed the Wyvern, that's what he was. He'd been patrolling often; more often than anyone else in the pride, actually.

"No."

He left it at that, which meant that more silence

ensued, with his face so close she could feel his breath on her naked breast.

Blushing like a teenager, she looked around the unfamiliar setting. She was in a large, simple room, much more spacious than the one she'd occupied at the inn. The eastern wall was entirely made of reflective glass, and her eagle approved, enjoying the view, even in the dark.

Someone had removed her jacket, and it lay on a white dresser, next to her shoes and pants.

She'd been naked around other people since she'd first shifted at age thirteen, so about half of her life. It had never been an issue. Right now, she had to fight her instinct to cross her arms across her chest. Not because she didn't want him to look at her, exactly... but she felt so damn self-conscious.

"Then why isn't your healer taking care of me?"

"We killed her a few days ago." Her mouth fell open. "She's the reason we had so many enemies at our door."

She'd betrayed her pride, then. Ava's eyes clouded as she remembered those who'd risen against her flock.

Not everyone had joined them, but the Enforcers had killed all those who spoke against them.

She closed her eyes, willing herself to stop thinking of it.

"Good."

The bitch had deserved to die, just like her old enforcers did.

The tiger chuckled low. "Good? What if she had her reasons?"

Ava shrugged. "You had kids, and she sent an army against you, regardless. There's no reason that could justify that. How did you get out of it, by the way?"

Her mind went directly to Knox. Had he been there? Was he still around?

"You've heard of Scions?" the tiger asked, and she rolled her eyes.

Had she ever.

"I'm from Italy. Most Scions are still based around Rome and Athens, you know. Except the Scandinavian lot, I guess."

She bit her lip, wondering if she'd said too much. Damn her stupid babble mouth.

"Italy? You don't speak with a Mediterranean accent." He replied. "If anything, you sound British."

She forced a smile. "British mother."

At least she wasn't lying. She just didn't add that her Russian, her Spanish, her French, and her Chinese also had no trace of Italian.

She may not have been raised to run for her life, but blending in, making foreign dignitaries comfortable, that had been drilled into her early and often.

"Anyway, you were saying about Scions?"

He was frowning when he explained they'd received help from their kind, perhaps not understanding just how rare that was. Scions were as selfish as they were self-centered. Which was understandable, because well, they *were* deities.

"They'll ask for a favor in exchange one day," she said, and the tiger nodded, not questioning her.

"All done."

She looked down to her bandage. It was probably overkill; he'd wrapped it all around her torso, breasts included.

Now that he was done, he sat up, and took a step away from her. She felt the absence in a way that made her question her sanity. Like he'd removed a part of her. Which was point-blank ridiculous.

"As soon as I get out of this door, my Alphas are going to ask me about you. I'll tell them I owe you, and they'll agree to let you stay for the night."

She nodded.

"Thank you. You didn't owe me anything. I was just..."

"I did, and now my debt is repaid," he replied, interrupting her.

Pain flashed through her, a pain that wasn't caused by her stupid wound. He was being nice about it, at least; he could have told her to get out of here right away.

"So," the shifter carried on, "if you want to stay come morning, you're going to have to come up with a story. A good story. Preferably the truth."

She opened her mouth and closed it. The truth. Telling them the truth right away wasn't only trusting them with her life; it was trusting them with the lives of all her kind. Could she do that?

"Rest up. I'll bring some broth in a bit. You have time. Just not much of it."

He turned on his heels as she bit her lip. Before he'd opened the door, Ava stopped him, suddenly aware of an embarrassing detail. She'd observed him for weeks, but...

"Hey?" she called. When he turned back to her, she asked, "What's your name?"

Eagles had keen vision, but there was no way she could have caught what he was actually saying from high up in the sky.

His eyes softened a bit. Ava watched, dazzled and practically shocked as he smiled. She hadn't seen him smile, not like that, not even to the children. It was like someone had suddenly lit a candle in the darkness.

"Coveney. Coveney Walker. I'm the Head Enforcer here."

DISOBEDIENCE

*C*oveney made his way to Rye's office as soon as he was done taking care of Ava, knowing the Alpha was running out of patience.

He'd looked at him without uttering a word when he'd brought the naked woman into the pride house. Rygan was kind like that. He could have just told him to get out, or to let her bleed out on their doorstep.

Rain had offered to take care of her, of course. He'd shaken his head.

"I still have some of the salve left that you made for me. I can do it, it's the same poison," he explained, all the while knowing it wasn't actually an explanation.

In the absence of a healer, now that Ola was gone to hell where she deserved to be, their witch ally was indubitably the best person to take care of a wounded patient. But Ava didn't know Rain.

She doesn't know you, either.

He shut up the voice in his mind and got to work, cleaning her wound until she woke up.

Coveney didn't have an explanation. He should be done with her. Now that she was safe, she should be inconsequential to him. Everyone else was. He owed Rye, Kim, Christine, and Ian. He'd spent enough years with Daunte and Jas to have developed some sort of affinity with them. He liked the kids. That was it.

Yet this stranger made him pace and mutter, wonder and worry, like nothing and no one else ever had, even before he'd become the cold, single-minded motherfucker he was.

Maybe he *should* let Rain have a crack at her. Witchcraft could very well be the issue there.

The Alphas were waiting for him; Rye sat behind his desk, Ace standing at his side. They hadn't doubted he'd come, because, well, that was just who he was.

Rye was still glaring in silence, his eyes bright, and the mating marks peeking from under his clothing blazing. Yeah, he was pissed. Ace, however, just seemed curious.

"I gave you a clear order," the Alpha male finally said, an edge to his voice.

Coveney bobbed his head, taking a seat. "And I willfully disobeyed." Which did support his theory: some witchcraft may be going on here. "I will accept the consequences. Demote me if you have to." His heart practically gave out, but he also added, "I'd understand if you banished me."

Aisling snorted. "Yeah, that's not going to happen, Coveney. Neither. You're the best at what you do, and Rye and I know just how lucky we are to have a workaholic like you at your post."

She said all that while pointedly looking at her mate, who sighed, dropping some of his glowering.

"That's right," he admitted. "Which is why acting like that is *definitely* not like you. Speak."

He wanted an explanation. Great. How could he spell it out for his Alphas when he didn't even know what made him act like a bloody lunatic?

"I told you she saved me," he replied. "I figured she might have been hit. I couldn't..." he stopped talking, knowing how lame it all sounded. "There's no excuse. I disobeyed."

Ace rolled her eyes.

"Oh, drop the crap. Rye was in an overprotective

mindset, or he would have sent you after her right away. Without her warning, we might all be dead right now. She helped us save *our son,* and the rest of our pride. I'm sorry I hadn't heard about all this before, or I would have intervened."

The Alpha male's shoulders finally relaxed, and he nodded curtly.

"I'm not used to you challenging my authority," he told him, pausing for a beat before he carried on. "But it's good to see you'll do it if you think it's right."

Wait, what? He messed up, and got *praised* for it? Today was so weird. Rye didn't hand over compliments every other day; on the contrary, he always looked at Coveney with something akin to disappointment.

"Still," the Alpha went on, "It doesn't change the fact that we don't know nearly enough about that girl to have her in our pride house, under the same roof as our kids. There's a reason why I sent the rest of our potential members to Ace's old place."

"She's wounded," Coveney pleaded, tense.

He thought about banishing Ava to one of the outer homes, by herself, vulnerable. Now that the potential members had been fully accepted in the pride, they'd be living with them, which meant she'd be well and truly alone there.

"Shifter healing is pretty quick."

"This poison will slow it down. I cleaned my wounds after minutes; hers have been festering for hours. I'll take responsibility for her. If you need to send her away, I'll go with her. But I'd prefer to have our resources at hand while she gets better."

Whatever Rye was about to say was cut off by Ace. "I'm good with that. If you're happy to take responsibility for her."

Coveney couldn't recall ever having been responsible for a person, on a one-on-one basis. He had a responsibility to the pack, and he saw to everyone's safety, but this seemed so different. Still, he acquiesced.

Before he left the office, he glanced at his Alphas again, and felt a little weirded out. He didn't chat away like everyone else did, and he stayed at a distance from the rest of the pride, but he saw and understood more than he let on. After what had happened to him, he'd started to pay a lot more attention to people: their expressions, the things they didn't say.

He'd seen Daunte's thing for his new mate, Clari, long before either of them had seen fit to do a thing about it. He'd wondered whether Ace could be Rye's mate very early on, catching something eerie about the way they glanced at each other.

Now, he saw something, too, as easily as if there had been a dialog bubble atop Ace's head. The Alpha female was cooking up something. She had a plan in mind, and it involved him.

He narrowed his eyes. He didn't think the woman had any reason to dislike him, so he might be over-reacting.

But he'd been wrong before.

THE ALPHA

*S*he woke up feeling like a shark had set its jaws around her middle and refused to let go. The slightest movement hurt, and her bandages were bloodstained.

On her bedside table, there was a full glass of water, and a bowl of something that looked like soup. She recalled Coveney saying he'd bring broth; obviously, he was a man of his word. He hadn't woken her up for it, and she was pretty grateful. Being conscious sucked. She hadn't been in pain while she slept, at least.

Her throat was dry, and her mouth felt downright disgusting, so she moved to grab the drink.

Shit. Wrong decision. She wasn't moving again - ever.

"Let me get that for you."

She froze.

The light was dim - it was clearly the middle of the night - but she should have heard him, sensed him. There was a stranger in her room, sitting on an armchair not too far from her, and it hadn't been the first thing she'd seen. Some shifter she was. She should have noticed him immediately.

Coveney brought the glass to her lips and tilted it slightly to let her take a sip.

She groaned, before managing to croak, "Thank you."

"Save your strength," he replied, apparently not one for pleasantries.

Good. It wasn't like she was up for a discussion right now.

"I need to look at the wound. The balm I put in there will prevent you from healing."

She narrowed her eyes and tensed, ready to bolt. That explained why she felt like she'd been run over, but why would he use something like that?

"To make sure your skin doesn't regrow over the poison," he explained, wincing. "Sorry. I'm not used to... speaking to people."

"You're part of a pride," she retorted, confused.

He shrugged. As she carried on staring, the tiger sighed, reading her annoyingly communicative silence. "You want me to clarify myself."

"Yep."

Unexpectedly, she saw him smile again.

"Well, there's that. No one expects me to explain myself these days."

She stared again, until he chuckled.

"A long time ago," he said, while undoing her bandage with care, "something happened that pissed me off. A lot. I stopped talking for a while after. I just couldn't speak because I felt like I was going to yell and explode, but the people around me were my friends, and they didn't deserve it. I started speaking again after a few months. I guess they were relieved, so they never pushed it afterwards. It suited me. I don't really..." he paused. "I don't have much to say to people."

His callused hands caressed her skin, and the pain became irrelevant, just like it had the day before, for an instant.

Needing a distraction, she asked, "What happened?"

His jaw set, and he kept it shut.

"If you don't want to tell me, you don't have to. But you need to say '*I don't want to tell you.*'"

"I don't mind telling you," he replied. "It's just going to take a second. I've never talked of it."

Were those butterflies in her tummy? Yep. Yep, they were.

"I was accused of rape." *Oh shit.* "Falsely," he clarified immediately. "And I was cleared since. Almost lost my neck, though. But I was young, and there wasn't enough proof, so I was banned from my pride instead. The friends I didn't want to yell at are those who left the pride with me and formed this one."

Oh, well. That explained why he didn't feel like being an ass to them. Still.

"That must be hard on you. Talking, communicating... I guess people are different, but that's how you know you're part of a community. Especially as a shifter. We need to feel like we belong. Talk, touch..." she trailed off again, because talking about touching him stirred something a little too intense for the circumstances.

Besides, she wasn't saying anything he didn't know.

"I don't touch people, either," he added, which only served to make his hand feel hotter against her. "It looks better. I'll clean the balm off, so you can heal up naturally."

He was very meticulous, and very thorough, too. He didn't even comment when her damn nipples got hard. Although he did bite back a grin.

"How do you feel?"

"Better already."

She could feel the healing process kicking in now; it made her sleepy, achy, and hot. *Yeah, right.* The hot part was all due to the fact that she was healing.

Liar.

"Good. I'll let you rest."

He returned to the armchair next to the large bed, and grabbed a book from the floor.

When she woke up later, the room bathed in morning light, he was still there, looking down at her.

❧

*B*reathe, Ava. Just breathe.

They were all there. All the larger than life shifters she'd seen from a distance. The room looked much smaller when they occupied it, expectantly staring at her.

51

Coveney had gone to fetch his Alphas, but he'd also brought his Beta back.

"Will you give us a minute?" Aisling Wayland-Cross asked, and although she'd formulated it as a question, everyone nodded, heading towards the door - everyone except Coveney. The Alpha female turned towards the Head Enforcer, clarifying, "That wasn't a suggestion."

Ava admired the Alpha's ways. She'd noticed it when she'd seen the pride interacting in the past, and it was evident now. Aisling wasn't one to wave her dominance left and right; she respected her pride, and it showed.

Visibly reluctant, the tiger turned on his heels, and closed the door behind him.

Finding herself alone with the Alpha, Ava felt the strength of her gaze a little harder. The woman was downright terrifying; yet for some reason, she didn't feel too uncomfortable in her company.

"I don't know much about eagle shifters - your kind stay pretty secluded – but, from what I've heard, you take your honor very seriously."

Ava nodded cautiously. That was one way of saying it. Pride was absolutely everything to their race.

"So much so that when someone loses their pride,

they often kill themselves. It's also not uncommon for Alphas to condemn whole families for the sins of one."

So much for not knowing much about eagles; she'd nailed their custom.

"Cats aren't like that," Aisling assured her. "No one here would judge you for someone else's crime."

Ava still felt uncomfortable, because she could have said as much in front of her pride. Yet she'd asked them to leave.

"But that's not what I wanted to say," the Alpha added. "See, I'm not like them."

She waved her hand towards the door, including all of her pride in the gesture.

"I don't have the same moral compass. My brain doesn't work the same way. I took your thumbprints and your DNA while you slept, and I got someone to track everything about you. I'm sure the report will be waiting on my desk."

Well, shit.

"You know why I did it?"

Of course she did - she'd wanted to know if she was a threat to their pride.

"Because you saved my kid yesterday. You warned

us, and, given the fact that we had our asses practically handed to us in mere minutes, without that heads-up, we'd all be dead. That means I'll work out who you're running from. I'll hunt them down, and I'll slit their throat."

She was matter-of-fact, conversational.

"I'm not what people would call civilized, or sane, for that matter. I'm saying that even if *you* did something, I would have your back. Understood?"

Actually, she didn't understand, not really. That wasn't how the world worked. But the Alpha female wasn't lying, she was sure of it. Shifters could feel, almost smell, blatant lies.

"You're saying you want me to trust you. And the thing is, I don't actually have any choice," she sighed. It was always going to come down to that. "You may want to call your mate back in for this bit."

So, a minute later, the five dominant shifters looked at her intently again, ready to listen to her explanation; the Alpha and Beta pairs, and Coveney made for a pretty intimidating audience. Clearing her throat, she wondered where she could start.

Her story hadn't started six months ago. It hadn't even started twenty-six years ago, when she'd been born.

"This is going to be a long tale, but I don't think there's any shortcut. I'd appreciate if you could keep the questions until the end, so I can stay on track."

There were nods all around.

"You're probably not going to believe a word of what I'm about to say, but this is the truth as I know it."

Shit.

Here goes nothing.

"A little under two thousand years ago, there was a mad, selfish man at the head of the most powerful empire in the world. Nero, he was called. He did many things, but one, the citizens of Rome never forgave. He took a humongous territory that belonged to the people, and made it his. His palace, his playground, his gardens.

"Finally, though, he died. Those left to pick up the pieces had a pretty hard road ahead. The government had lost the faith of the people, and regaining it was going to take a lot of work.

"Then Flavian rose to power and decided to give that land back to the people. You've seen the results in postcards, I'm sure. They call it the Colosseum nowadays.

"This is common knowledge. What most don't know is that Vespasian Flavia, and the rest of his family, were shifters.

"Financing the amphitheater wasn't easy. *Giving* it to the people meant that they Couldn't raise the funds from taxes, for one. So they went to war, heading east, to Jerusalem.

"They won, bringing back gold, of course, but they also brought back slaves. A lot of them. Only three were of consequence, though.

"We don't know if they're related. We don't know their actual names. They never spoke to their captors, according to the records we have of those days. What we know is that they were seen as rulers by the rest of the slaves. What we know is that they also were shifters. Wolves.

"Titus Flavia was so proud at having caught such a powerful, distinguished enemy. Wolf shifters had founded Rome - think back to the story of Romulus and Remus, and connect the dots - and now here they were, at his mercy.

"The Flavian amphitheater wasn't ready yet, but there were others where gladiators fought. He took them there and pitted them against each other, first. When they wouldn't fight, he threw animals at them. They massacred them without effort. But, relentlessly, every fortnight, he threw them in the pit and watched them fight. In between, instead of training them and polishing them, like other gladiators, he starved them to ensure they would ultimately die.

"It took years, I'm told. Finally, though, one of them fell. And the moment he stopped breathing, hundreds, if not thousands, of slaves died, too.

"They weren't sure about what happened, at first. Had they all committed suicide to commiserate with their master? It seemed unlikely. Titus needed to understand, so he had another one executed - a female, I think.

"As she died, other hundreds of slaves were lost. This was quite a blow for all of Rome, and it terrified Titus. As a shifter himself, he wanted to understand what caused it. He went to the last wolf and made him an offer. Tell me, he said, and I'll grant you your freedom. He didn't believe it, but at long length, and probably after a fair bit of torture, Fenrir finally spoke.

"He told Titus the legend of the first wolves, one red, one white, one gray. They'd been turned together, and every single werewolf in the world had either been bred, or turned by them.

"Fenrir said he was the direct descendant of the First Gray wolf. The last descendant. His companions had been the last of the First Red and Arctic wolves. Without that original bloodline, without anyone in the world with First blood running through their veins, they were all doomed.

"Titus laughed, relieved and victorious. He knew he came from First blood, too. As they'd never turned anyone, every Eagle shifter alive shared his blood. He wasn't likely to ever be afflicted. But it gave him ideas. Realizing there could be power in having thousands of followers who would die if something happened to him, he started to turn more humans into shifters.

"He lost interest in Rome, and faked his death just as the Amphitheater was built. Humans were of no consequence now. Finding the best witches, he took an island and made it his. The money stolen in Jerusalem hadn't run out yet, so he used that to make his Dale.

"He died eventually, of course, but his descendants were a little less egocentric, or so I like to think. Still, they saw that he hadn't had the worst idea, especially after the new religion came. Humans destroyed every reminder of their old faith as best they could over the following centuries, in the name of their new savior.

"Not in Dale, though. Our wards have stood for two thousand years, and we still have marble halls and columns so tall they seem to touch the sky.

"I'm Ava Flavia Dale. Six months ago, our people started to question the old stories. I frankly understand why, because it sounds like old mumbo jumbo to me, too. But they massacred most of my family. I ran east, as my brother went north to get them off my trail.

"Before we went our separate ways, he asked me to try to find the only person who can give us a true account of what happened all those years ago. He told me to find Fenrir. There's a good chance the Enforcers who betrayed us are right, of course. But, if they aren't, if killing us means the end of our kind, we need to know. So, the idea is to find him, and ask him if it's true. Then, in case it is, I guess I need to convince him to testify under a truth spell, so that this madness can end."

WITCHCRAFT

*T*here was a long silence after that speech. Everyone was staring at Ava, who seemed fixated on her nails like they were the most fascinating thing she'd ever seen.

Coveney didn't doubt her story. Not because it wasn't insane - it most definitely was. He just didn't think she was lying. Some shifters were trained to, of course, but it wasn't easy. Their kind weren't as astute as wolves, but they could still smell if someone started sweating, or see the slightest change in expression.

"But if it all happened thousands of years ago..." Ace started.

"Fenrir is still alive," Ava replied, anticipating her question. "Everything else may be a children's tale, who knows? But that part is definitely true. There's a wolf who's lived since then, he doesn't even make his trail hard to find. He's a known benefactor to his kind. These past few centuries, he's even helped other shifters." She bit her lip, before confessing, "I applied to this pride when I heard that he'd been in touch to help you a while back. I just need a way to contact him that won't end with my head on a spike because of my surname."

So, she'd wanted to use them. Coveney turned to Rye, searching his expression. There was a chance the Alpha might have taken that admission as an offense. But the poor guy just looked like he was developing a headache, like the rest of them.

Catching everyone's expressions, he realized something. Shit. If she *was* telling the truth, and if the tales she grew up hearing hadn't just been some stupid myth invented by a power-hungry family, their lifelines were linked to someone out there. They needed to find out, pronto.

"Helped us?" Daunte asked, confused.

Ava bobbed her head.

"Yeah. He doesn't go by Fenrir, of course. Not really inconspicuous nowadays, I guess. Although Knox is hardly any better, really."

Knox.

All the Wyverns turned to Ace, staring at her expectantly. Her mouth hung open for a beat, then she just laughed, so hard she had to hold her sides.

"Wait, you're telling me *Knox* is that old super werewolf? As in, Knox, the obnoxious loner?"

Ava shrugged. "I think so. I might be wrong, but..."

"Oh, no," Ace replied, vehemently shaking her head. "If you're not insane, you're definitely not wrong. It's just so fucking typical. Basically, you're right. He really doesn't hide it."

On that confusing note, she pulled her phone out, and started playing with it.

"Wait, what are you doing? We have to discuss this..."

"Yada, yada, yada," she rolled her eyes at her mate. "Conclusion of the pointless discussion: we need to call him and get his ass down here. We had this whole episode with Tria just a few weeks back. I'm just fast-forwarding the process."

Ava was seriously chewing at her lip. Coveney moved without thinking, cupping her face, and running his thumb over the red lower lip.

"Don't do that," he growled at her. If anyone was going to bite those lips, it was him. "It'll be just fine."

He didn't have to look at them to feel his pridemates staring.

"Did I miss something?" Daunte whispered, before groaning when someone - probably his mate, or Ace - elbowed his stomach.

"Okay, we need to speak to the rest of the pride," the Alpha female said. "And my parents. And everyone I fucking know. If there's a First Shifter family in the feline world, we need to learn what we can. You get better," she added, addressing Ava, no doubt.

Although Coveney didn't see her, because he was still looking right into the eagle's eyes.

They were so strange. Purple, almost.

"And, Coveney, you're in charge of her, so your usual duties..."

"I'm taking some of my time off," he retorted.

A short silence ensued.

"Right. That makes sense. Alien abduction."

"Shut it, Daunte," Ace retorted. "And let's get out of here."

He'd thank the woman later for that. He'd wanted and needed them all gone.

Fuck, what was she doing to him? The girl was a

small thing; five foot two at most, but packing one hell of a punch.

He wanted her, that much had been clear at first glance. That part, he understood. He was a goddamn shifter; it might have started late for him, but he still wanted sex just like the rest of them.

He didn't get the rest, though. He didn't get why he felt the need to touch her, touch her lips, even in front of other people. Public displays of affection weren't part of his M.O. Affection wasn't part of his M.O. He didn't understand why he needed her to stop worrying about Knox. Why he needed her to believe there was nothing to worry about, because he'd be right there, next to her, and ready to lunge at the wolf - immortal or not - if he made a wrong move towards her.

So, he was back to pondering about witchcraft.

"How's the wound?" he asked.

Her cheeks heated up as she lowered the bedding to let him see her torso. He took in the angry red patch of skin, which had done a complete 180 in a few hours, then went a little higher, to look at her breasts. They weren't huge, just a handful, but standing proudly, firm as fuck. The dark nipples were practically begging to play.

But she was self-conscious, more so than shifters

usually were. He found it both endearing and strange, because the woman was gorgeous. The dark blond, highlighted waves, the fucking purple eyes, and the curves she'd managed to pack on her slim frame must have turned heads wherever she went.

"Better. Good. I guess I should think about getting you clothes now," he commented out loud, which surprised him.

As he'd told her, he really wasn't a talker.

But she wanted him to talk, she'd said as much. So, he did. Although it seemed irrelevant.

Witchcraft...

"Yeah. Clothes would be nice."

He tilted his head. "Still thinking about it."

Ava laughed, shaking her head as she pulled the covers back. "You're definitely a guy."

He was. An interested guy. But she was wounded, and frightened, so, however much he wanted to say he was going to make her scream his name and claw at his back, he didn't.

"You think you're up to getting out of there yet? I can bring some food up..."

"But if you do, the rest of the pride will think I'm

hiding." She grimaced, making it clear that she didn't like that. "I can get up."

Coveney tilted his head, curious.

"You're hard to place. You're pretty shy, and could use a confidence boost, but I don't read a clear submissive vibe from you. Plus, you've applied as a fighter, or you wouldn't have been called a few weeks back."

Rye had asked a bunch of candidates to join him; people with fighting skills. Expecting the battle that had taken place the previous day, he hadn't wanted to involve more members who needed protection.

"I'm dominant," she nodded. "Just not *very* dominant. My animal makes up for it, though."

"You let her do the fighting?" he asked, without judging her. A lot of shifters relied on their animal.

To his surprise, Ava shook her pretty head. "No, not often. She's kick-ass, but in a one-on-one, I fight. I'm not that good. Never won against one of my siblings, not even once. But still, I was trained. Not too badly either, or I wouldn't have made it out of Dale alive."

Dale. One of the million bombs she'd launched at them over the last hour.

"There's really a whole place that looks like ancient Rome, then?"

She shrugged. "Not completely. It *is* the twenty-first century, you know. We even have Wi-Fi. But, yeah, the architecture is still intact, and we have plenty of relics. Except, they aren't all dusty and ruined like those they keep in the museums."

Mind blowing.

"I'd like to see that someday."

She sighed. "I think some part of me would like to see it again. But even if they all stop actively trying to murder me, I'm never returning to the flock. Most of the members of my family died before my eyes. I'm done with Dale."

BREAKFAST

The house was lovely. Very modern, the polar opposite to the place where she'd grown up, but over the last few months she'd seen plenty of modern edifices, and she could recognize that this one was far superior to the norm. The curved staircases, carved ceilings, and the materials - metals and polished stone - made it obvious it had been designed to stand out. It was also large; she'd seen it from outside, but it was even more evident when seeing the indoors. Twisting her neck to see up the staircase, and looking down again, she commented, "this is a pretty big place."

"We fit in nicely, and there's fifteen of us. Eight adults, nine kids. The kids share - there are two of them per room, and Niamh, the oldest, stays by herself. We've added three newbies recently, so that leaves two guest rooms." He frowned. "Rye said he plans to see more potential recruits soon, so we're going to have to either expand, or see if any of us want to leave the main house."

Ava bit her lip. It didn't sound like they had the capacity for too many new members. Would they let her stay? Doubtful, especially if Fenrir contradicted the old text. She'd still be wanted by her flock, who controlled every eagle out there. And it wasn't like she was bringing a lot to the table. Richard, Aria, or Rupert would have been another story. Aria had been strong - so strong she could punch through walls. Rupert's thing had been speed. Richard was the best of them, at *everything*. She was the lesser Dale, the softer one, too.

She hadn't lied to Coveney: she could take care of herself, but that was about it.

They arrived at the first floor; she could hear the buzz in the next room stop before they walked in. A dozen pairs of eyes were pinned on her when Coveney led her to the living room.

She recognized most of them. There were a couple of unfamiliar females sitting next to Ace, but she'd seen the others plenty of times.

Ava wasn't surprised to find that most of the glances ranged from suspicious to downright hostile.

She bit her lip. The second she did, an oh-so-familiar hand she shouldn't already be used to circled her waist. "I sit over this way," Coveney said. "It will be a squeeze. We need a bigger table."

The shifters she hadn't met yet all looked like their Head Enforcer had grown a tail and horns, staring at him in shock.

He pulled out a chair, and got her to sit at what was obviously his place, content to stand next to her.

"You've met Rye, Ace, Daunte, and Clari. This is Rain, the witch who made the salve that healed you."

She waved in the direction of the mocha-skinned beauty at Ace's right, who smiled and waved back. "And Vivicia. She helped me track you down."

"The wolf," Ava guessed, wondering if every female he knew were that stunning.

But she wasn't jealous. Because that would be point-blank idiotic. Right?

"Christine is our cook," he pointed to a brunette who'd crossed her arms on her chest when they'd first walked in, but she was now too busy staring at Coveney. "Ariadna and Theo, two newcomers. Luke, Ian, and Jas are probably patrolling."

"That's right. Luke is taking an Enforcer crash-course and covering your shifts," Daunte retorted.

"And those're our kids. Lola," he indicated a rosy cheeked toddler, "Niamh, Jasper, Clive, Will, Victoria, Daniel, Hsu, and the source of all the trouble from yesterday, Zack."

"Hello little Zack," she waved, as the adorable baby was intently staring at her.

He immediately moved his plump little arms towards her, kicking his feet to make his intentions known. The woman who carried him, Vivicia, glanced towards the Alpha before crossing the room, and handing him to Ava.

"Oh, just look at you," she gushed.

"Careful with the neck," Vivicia cautioned, but Ava took him with ease.

She was used to kids - kissing babies was the soft Dale's job. Thankfully, she also happened to like them.

"I got this," she said, and, of course, the child decided to prove her wrong.

Shocking the heck out of her, he shifted right there in her arms, turning into a spotted little cat in an instant. She adjusted her arms, and managed not to drop him.

"He bites," the Beta female warned her, making a few people chuckle or roll their eyes.

Ava tilted her head.

"Clari was recently turned by Zack," he explained.

Well, that explained so much. "That's why the council went after you."

"Yes. The issue should be resolved now, though. Coffee?"

"Hot water and lemon, if you have it?"

Coveney stepped away, heading towards the kitchen, and came back with her drink. As her hands were taken, he also asked what she wanted to eat, and loaded her plate with bacon and pancakes from platters on the table.

"Let me take him, so you can eat," Ace offered, holding her hands up to receive the kitten, but it had decided that playing with her hair was far too interesting, and, if she so much as shifted, his little claws grabbed her arm.

She sighed. The damn thing couldn't have been more irresistible, but she was hungry, verging on hangry.

Coveney chuckled, before holding her fork up to allow her to eat some food.

By the time the kitten had fallen asleep, Coveney'd fed her the entire plate.

"Thank you. I was genuinely starving."

"I'm always ravenous after healing, too."

Oh. She then recalled he'd also been hit. More than her.

"Are you okay? You had a bunch of arrows in your flanks by the time I left."

"Rain sorted me out."

"Still, you must be hungry. Take your seat back."

She got up, and went to give the child back to his mother.

Now Coveney was occupying his place, she looked around awkwardly; there were no other chairs around the table. She considered going to the dining room area and sitting on one of the sofas, but some-thing - madness, perhaps - made her think better of it. Straightening her spine, and doing her best to ignore the glances, she went right back where she'd been intending to stand next to Coveney, just like he'd done when she'd been in his place. But he shifted in his seat to allow for some room, and pulled at her hand until she got the hint.

Oh.

She felt her cheeks flush as she dropped onto his lap.

The man carried on eating, occasionally feeding her

from his plate, as her heart beat a thousand miles an hour and her mind raced.

She wasn't used to felines. She wasn't familiar with the Wyverns. Maybe it was nothing. Maybe they were just that tactile with everyone.

But she recalled him clearly saying *I don't touch people.*

She was probably just being silly. But she couldn't shut up the voice that whispered that it felt like he was claiming her in front of all his pridemates.

THE INTRUDER

*A*va went back to bed after breakfast, and, reluctantly, he left her to it, this time. He just wanted to sit next to her until she was better, but he had another instinct, just as strong.

After everything she'd said, he needed to make sure she was safe.

Every member of the pride got paid a salary for their contribution. He used his for clothing, when he needed something new, and a phone, occasionally. That was about it. Over the years, a healthy amount had added up.

Still, he wasn't sure how to contact the best private investigators out there, so he started researching it. He would have preferred to do it from his room, as

Ava slept in his bed, but, as he didn't own his own computer, he used the Enforcer office, across the hall from Rye's.

Somehow, everyone had seen necessary to converge on that very room this morning. And they were looking at him. Or talking to him.

Nosy idiots.

"What the ever -fucking hell happened to you, man? It's aliens, isn't it? Just tell me. I can deal. If there're body snatchers around, wink twice. I know you're in there, mate."

He just rolled his eyes, ignoring Daunte.

"I know I'm majorly pussy whipped, but it's been less than twenty-four hours, and you're practically wiping her ass for her. Come on, this is..."

"She's probably my fated mate," Coveney said conversationally, without bothering to lift his head from the computer he was working on.

He'd guessed as much the instant he'd seen her. Every second he spent in her presence made that theory seem more likely. Finally, feeling slightly annoyed at all the staring, he lifted his head.

It wasn't just Daunte; Vivicia and Theo had also stopped pretending to look for something in his files, and were busy catching flies.

"What?"

"You know how rarely fated mates find each other? I mean, it's not impossible, but two pairs in one pride would be insane."

Insane or not, that was his reality. He wasn't going to tell her until he was one hundred percent sure, but, right now, everything pointed to that theory. The way she felt so perfect against him. The way he wanted to bend his very soul to accommodate her. Every instant away from her seemed endless, and when she was near he wanted, needed, her closer.

Oh, and he wanted her. How he wanted her. He hadn't so much as breathed a word about it, because if he voiced it, if he so much as flirted, or tried to act on it, he didn't think he could hold himself back.

He needed to, though. That wound on her side was getting better, but she'd received it just a day ago. A human would have taken a month to recover; she'd be fine by tomorrow. Until then, he couldn't, wouldn't think about her luscious little body. Or her perfect tits.

He forced himself to remain seated.

"Maybe that's because most shifters don't meet anyone from other communities, or other countries. Still, the word *fated* suggests that life does set up a chance encounter. It's just a matter of recognizing it for what it is."

They seemed to digest that. Finally, Daunte nodded slowly. "Okay, I'll buy that. Still. You know how long it took Rye to work out that Ace was his?"

Coveney shrugged. "He didn't analyze the information in front of him right away, is all. I actually guessed she might be his, the second time I saw you together. I figured she and Rye would catch on in their own time."

It had seemed obvious to him.

"You looked as surprised, when we found them..."

"Because they had weird, glowing marks, and their eyes were bright as neon signs. That part, I hadn't anticipated."

He returned to his work, hoping that was the last of the distractions.

"Exactly how smart are you?" Daunte asked, making him smile.

He may or may not have graduated with a Master's online at nineteen. The initial members of the pride knew that. They'd just forgotten it, or forgotten what it meant. Back when he had been a different person, before his banishment, he used to love solving puzzles, winning chess games in a few moves. Just because he was now their muscle didn't mean he didn't still have the highest IQ in the pride, at 144. They'd tested him in middle school, because he'd been so bored they'd figured he could stand to jump a few classes.

He knew better than to tell that to Daunte, though. The man would never leave it alone if he knew. Coveney just shrugged.

"Ace made a few calls already. The Flavia Dale are pretty big in Europe. Like, royalty big, amongst the shifters. They get visits from government officials; Rye's father, our goddamn king, said they're huge. If she manages to prove her family was right, if this whole First story is true, she might get back to her place, you know."

He didn't actually. Recalling how she'd said she was done with Dale, he doubted it.

"What will you do, then? You'd leave us?"

Everything in him recoiled at that very idea. If anyone had asked him whether he'd planned to leave the Wyverns yesterday, even while they were about to get massacred, his answer would have been *no, never*. He wouldn't even have hesitated.

Now, he frowned, and stayed silent, utterly torn.

"This is a pointless conversation. You're asking about the end of a movie as soon as the opening credits have rolled."

He was being vague as shit, because he honestly didn't have an answer. Daunte might very well have called him out on it, but, thankfully, they were interrupted.

They all felt it to their bones when their front door opened. They rushed out of the Enforcer office at the same time as Rye and Ace came out of theirs; Christine popped her head out from the living room.

They all stared in silence at the stranger who'd just pushed past their wards without activating them. He'd entered their home like it wasn't locked under deadbolts, simply pushing the door open.

The man seemed to be in his twenties, older than Daunte, a little younger than Coveney, perhaps. He had blond hair on the longer side; it fell in front of his cold, piercing grey eyes without bothering him.

Anywhere, he would have stood out; not only because he looked like a goddamn movie star, but his presence seemed strange, eerie. He wore a fitted suit, and, more remarkable yet, there was a cane in his hand, although he walked easily, without a limp. He used it at each step, though. Each slow, predatory step.

Ace crossed the room, her hand extended, smiling at him.

"Knox."

*H*e looked at the hand like he expected it to bite him, but, finally, placing his cane on the crook of his elbow, he shook it.

"Aisling. Still alive, I see."

He inclined his head respectfully. She rolled her eyes. "So, you've heard about our little issue with the council."

He smiled, and from the top of the stairs, Ava definitely saw a flash of his white teeth.

"Hearing things is what I do. I'm surprised you didn't think to come to me for aid," he challenged, lifting a brow.

Ace was absolutely non-apologetic. "There was a chance you might have wanted to join our enemies, and, quite frankly, I didn't need you enough to risk *that*."

The wolf chuckled low. "Clever woman. Now, I hear you have a little bird under your roof."

His cold, piercing gaze rose slowly, until he was looking right at her.

Shit.

Ava gulped, walking down the stairs.

Here was the man the legends talked of. There was no doubt that what they said of him was accurate enough. He looked like a killer, the kind who did it not because they needed to, but because it was fun.

He also looked like after killing, he'd fuck his way through every woman in his path. Covered in blood. While laughing like a maniac.

She shook her head. Well, that vision was quite specific.

"Ava Flavia Dale."

He said each of her names slowly, rolling it around his tongue.

She didn't flinch.

"Your sister was taller. Prettier, too."

Now, she was narrowing her eyes.

"They said she was stronger, yet you were the one who survived."

She glanced at Ace, wondering if she'd told him about her siblings; but none of what she'd told the Alpha would have given him a clue about Aria's height or her beauty.

He'd been observing them. Of course. Watching your enemies was smart.

Shit. Shit. Shit.

She controlled her breathing, and forced her body to appear calm, although she wanted to tremble, and maybe hide behind Coveney, who was waiting for her at the bottom of the stairs.

Finally, she'd reached the last step.

"I was lucky," she replied.

The wolf tilted his head. "Luck. Yes. It's certainly luck that allowed you to evade some of the most bloodthirsty hunters of the entire shifter kind for six months, I'm sure."

She wasn't surprised when he moved. Somehow, at the back of her mind, she'd always suspected it was inevitable.

The wolf seized the top of his cane and pulled it, unsheathing a long, thin sword, before he launched himself at her, still smiling broadly, like he was having a hell of a lot of fun.

The Wyverns didn't have a chance in hell of stopping him. They might be felines, but in their human shells, there was no way they could have matched his speed. They probably wouldn't have been able to do a damn thing even if they'd shifted.

Coveney, who was closest to her, attempted to push her behind him, but she didn't let him.

This wasn't his fight. And she wasn't going to let him get mauled to death for her.

So, she did what she had to do. Defense was pointless, pathetic against a predator such as him. She leaped on the nearest wall, and used her momentum to jump to his flanks. Her kick hit the mark. Holy fuck, she'd hit him! Thankfully, her body didn't let her mind slow it down. On automatic pilot, she punched his sword hand, and flipped back when he appeared at her other side, claws extended this time, although the rest of him remained human.

He could partially shift. He wasn't the only one.

She extended her wings and flew up just in time to avoid his bite, before folding them back, and grabbing the Malacca's sheath. He'd carelessly dropped it on the floor. Not a smart move.

She'd learned early that any weapon was better than no weapon; it might not have an edge, but the thin wooden cane allowed her to keep his sword and teeth at a distance.

She was breathing hard, and maybe even sweating, but it hit her, suddenly, when the sword only missed her by a hair.

Her eyes bulged. She didn't understand how or why, but she knew, without a doubt, that the wolf was just sparring.

All of a sudden, just as quickly as he's started, he stopped moving, drawing his sword back.

She was pacing, holding her side, hurting everywhere, but the wolf didn't have a hair out of place. He didn't even seem winded, damn it.

"Yeah," he chuckled. "You're a Flavian, alright."

The wolf extended his hand expectantly.

Slowly, reluctantly, she closed the distance she'd managed to create between them and shook it, still not quite sure what the hell was happening there.

"Nice try, birdie. But I just want my shaft back."

"Oh."

Feeling stupid, she handed him the damn sheath. He

could obviously kill her even if she kept it, anyway. He hadn't even tried.

"What was that all about? She's fucking healing," Coveney seethed, rushing to her side, and pulling her t-shirt high enough to check on her wound.

"I'm alright," she replied, although she also would have loved to know what the hell it had been all about.

The First Wolf smiled again.

"I heard women were made of something more in Dale. I had to check."

"Well, this one is taken," Coveney stated simply, holding her against him.

And he must have been utterly suicidal, because he went as far as throwing his dominant vibes at the First fucking Wolf. The two-thousand- year-old ex-gladiator who'd just moved like a fucking ninja without breaking a sweat.

Knox, Fenrir, or whatever he went by, tilted his head, and raised a brow, like he found Coveney's little display endearing.

"Is she now? Shame." He turned his back on them, disinterested. "Now, I sincerely hope you have some tea for me, dearest," he said, taking Aisling's arm, and letting her guide him to the dining room.

What. The...

"Did you just get into a pissing contest over me with an ancient, murderous, and potentially insane werewolf?"

"Looks like it."

Yeah, that's what she'd figured.

She attempted to looking forbidding. "I'm not a thing a guy can just claim, you know."

"I know," Coveney replied, still not offering any sort of apology, or letting her go, for that matter.

"You should..."

"You can stop talking now. I'm about to kiss you."

She had some sort of reply in mind, but the instant his lips found hers, she had no fucking clue what it might have been.

His lips were cool, yet everything in her burned when they touched her skin. She folded against him, wanting, needing more; her hands flew to his neck to ensure she could keep him there for the rest of time. But, just like that, he stopped, taking a step back.

"See? That's why you're taken," he said, winking playfully, before walking in the living room.

THE ENEMY

*A*va made no damn fucking sense. Shy. Skittish. Flying around like a goddamn ninja, faster than anyone he'd ever seen until today.

Which was hot. Very, very hot. And reassuring, too; he hadn't quite known what to do with that precious girl who looked like she might break. Turns out, she might be the one breaking him. With her little finger. Wearing a blindfold.

And, by the gods, her lips. Her soft, soft lips. What he would have given for another taste just then. But he knew, without a doubt, that he wouldn't have been able to stop himself if he'd given in, even just a little more, and they had issues to deal with right now. Like the weird-ass, Earl-Grey-tea- drinking wolf in their living room.

Knox sat in Rye's armchair, like he'd instantly known that it was the Alpha's place. He looked goddamn satisfied, as the females in the pride rushed around to serve him. Ace brought him his tea, and Clari offered him a cupcake.

He stared at the plate with some amusement before taking it.

"Why, thank you, Clarissa. I do have a sweet tooth, actually. Although it's a secret I generally keep close to my chest."

The perfectly happily mated Beta female blushed, making Daunte groan.

"Leave my poor pridemates alone, Knox," Ace admonished him, rolling her eyes. "You have enough females half in love with you across the globe already."

"Never," he replied. Then his easy smile disappeared, and his eyes flashed with something that made Coveney stop walking towards him and glance at Ava, ensuring she was at his side. "Now, I've wondered what would have you summon me here after your little bird chirped about all my secrets. So I looked into it. The slaughter of Dale."

His eyes burned holes at Ava.

"You need me to stop them hunting you," he stated.

Coveney tensed, wishing he could do something other than stand there. But Rye and Ace, the most dominant people he knew, seemed to be just as powerless. Both had moved to help Ava earlier; neither had made it to her before the wolf. Or before she could save her own ass.

"You need me to talk about the First lines."

"I don't know if it's true…"

"Yet you crossed half a world in the hope it may be."

Knox wasn't giving an inch. Another woman might have asked, or even begged, but Ava just stared at him, somehow knowing he'd already made his decision. He just seemed to enjoy making people squirm.

"Do you know what they did to me in Rome, little bird? Do you know I was tied up day and night? I pissed and shat in the corner of a small room. I think, over the ten years they had me, that corner was never cleaned. My wolf became feral. The only thing that kept us together was the fact that my human half was just as wild by that point. But I had to live."

"Your blood isn't your own," Ava said, amusing him.

"Quite. That was my saying. I heard you've made it your family motto. The Flavian always had good taste."

"So, it's true. If you died…"

"Every single werewolf on earth dies with me. Just as every eagle will, when you and this brother of yours meet your fate. Unless I *talk*."

It was obvious to Coveney than he had no intention to, not without a price, anyway. He was just taunting them.

"Knox, you're not that much of an asshole," Ace told him, making him chuckle.

"Oh, I am. I'd love nothing more than to see her kind disappear. I'd cheer as the eagles fell and drink to their enemies' health." After a beat, he added, "If I could afford to."

Coveney frowned, not sure what he meant.

"What you're not questioning is: what makes a group of people so willing to try out a theory that may very well mean their own doom?" he rolled his eyes. "Your enemies were manipulated. By someone who either wanted to confirm the importance of the First lines, or by someone who needed agles out of the way. Most probably both."

Shit, that made sense. Eagles *were* the most powerful allies of the shifter council, after all.

"The shifter council has plenty of enemies. Hell, yesterday, we figured amongst those. It makes sense."

"Certainly." Then, like it was common knowledge,

he added, "I founded the council. Its primary objective was to locate, and protect, every First line of our kind. Should the council fall, we'd all be at risk. Now, who do you think could possibly want to endanger every shifter in the entire world, hm?"

Fuck.

"Regulars."

*I*t had been decades since the sups had come out of the closet, but the reaction of regular humans had been to attack, right away. The vampires subdued them with ease, everyone knew that. Later, when other races had come out of the closet, they'd all seen hate groups rise, ganging up against the sups they could find.

The fanatics were rarely successful in their attempts to harm any of them; even the weakest, most submissive of shifters were stronger than most regulars. Witches, vampires, and the others could also take care of themselves.

But there were plenty of haters, they all knew that. That was why so many shifters never left their prides or packs; not wanting to deal with them. The regular human laws, drafted by the vampires who let them govern themselves, made it clear that shifters and other sups didn't answer to their laws. At least, as long as they didn't interfere with a regular. When a sup had to protect himself against normal humans, it often resulted in blood, and even when it was self-defense, the regulars came down on them, hard.

The whole dynamic was quite toxic, and everyone knew something needed to give. They talked about just being patient, showing the regulars they weren't monsters. Still, decades had passed without changing a thing, except in places like Lakesides.

If Knox was right, and regulars were behind what had occurred in Dale, there would never be peace. They'd all but declared war against their whole kind.

"Most regulars are indifferent to us; some may even like us. But there are others - not just the haters. Those who are simply resigned that we're stronger than them. If they saw a weakness, they'd pounce. Now, tell them that killing a few dozen of us is enough to rid the world of shifters..."

"We'd be royally fucked. All of us."

Perfect. Their day was just getting better and better.

"I may be mistaken," the wolf admitted. "But, regardless, the little bird will live."

WAITING

*A*va was probably insane, but after a little while, she relaxed around Knox. It might have to do with the fact that while she was pretty certain everything she'd heard about him was well-deserved, he seemed genuine. Under the swagger, the veiled threats, and the coldness, she saw wisdom, compassion, and...

"You know, you may just look as pretty as your late sister, if you put a couple of pounds on. Particularly around the tits and ass, little bird. Why women persist in resembling boys these days is completely beyond me."

Never mind. He was a dick.

"Of course, you'll breed soon. Perhaps you'll be fortunate enough to keep some baby weight."

"Oh, fuck off."

He beamed at her like she'd given him a present wrapped in a pretty bow.

"Are you going to contradict me, Ava Flavia of Dale? That you didn't immediately think of it when I told you the legends are true? You need a child - so does your brother. *Your blood isn't your own.*"

"Then why don't *you* have a litter of pups?" she retorted, before wincing.

Okay, so he'd walked into that one, but, if he hadn't had any kids over two thousand years, maybe he just couldn't.

"Not for lack of trying," he replied pleasantly, although his jaw tensed a little. "My spawn have the unfortunate tendency of attempting to cut their way out of their mothers, far too early and in the most inopportune of fashions. It's quite literally a bloody mess. Why, are you offering your womb?" he tilted his head. "Your boy may have a thing or two to say against it."

"How did you survive this long?" she mused in wonder. "Everyone who meets you *must* hate your guts."

Her tongue was loosened by the fact that she didn't think he'd chop her head off now.

"I grow on people."

"Like fungus."

"And if that fails, I also happen to be able to kill just about anyone with an embarrassing lack of effort."

She rolled her eyes. Show off.

At least, bickering with him helped pass the time while they waited. It beat twiddling her thumbs.

K nox hadn't agreed with her plan; going to her flock and testifying seemed to play into their enemies' hands, according to him.

"Think of it. They'd still walk away with information we'd very much like to keep under wraps. And they *have* massacred your family, regardless. Wouldn't it be more fun to repay the favor?"

It wouldn't, actually. Just because a few people had risen against her family didn't mean that she wanted to go to war with the entire flock of Dale. Particularly since the rest of the eagles of the world might join in.

"Who do you think they'd follow? The traitors on your parents' seat, or a Flavia?"

"I don't know," she admitted.

She had never done anything to earn the loyalty of her kind; they didn't even know her. Shy as she was, she'd hidden from the limelight, avoiding large gatherings. Richard may have been another story, he'd travelled to each corner of the globe and made alliances.

"Well, how about we find out?"

The idea held merit, but she would have liked it more if it wasn't based on her ability to rally hundreds of freaking eagles because of the blood running in her veins.

She'd paced the room as the smug wolf got to work. She'd paced some more as answers came from the various Eagle Alphas.

Now she was done pacing, too busy feeling like she was going to throw up. Sixty-two. Sixty-two flocks had answered, within less than an hour. Sixty-two flocks out of the seventy-nine Knox had contacted had agreed to meet her, to see what she had to say.

Fuck.

"What if it's a trap? They could just want to get to me."

"It could be." Knox never said yes, or no, admitting that every possibility was plausible, which was nothing short of infuriating. "But I have my doubts. For one, they know I'll be there."

Cocky wolf.

Ava heard a noise, and turned to the door hopefully; but there was just an old cat of the non-shifting variety, leisurely licking his butt. He raised his spotted head, took one look at Knox, and started hissing.

The wolf sighed.

"You know, I'm incredibly fond of videos of kittens. Yet I've never seen one do anything remotely adorable in front of me. They're all spitting and hissing."

"That's called having good taste," she muttered, with a last glance at the door.

Where was he?

The Wyvern felines had left her with Knox, Rain, and Vivicia in the lounge, while they went out with their kids.

"They've been cooped up in here for too long," Rye had announced. "We're going for a run with them."

Coveney had attempted to stay behind, but the Alpha had been strict.

"There're too many children for us to handle in town with three of us on patrol," he'd told him. "And they won't listen to strangers the way they listen to you. You're coming."

In other words, the Wyverns were having a meeting of their own. They hadn't even been subtle about it. And who could blame them? She'd brought a pile of gooey shit to their doorstep hours after they'd survived their latest shit-storm.

And she *shouldn't* be so anxious to see Coveney walk back in, dammit. Yes, the guy wanted to fuck her. He'd made that clear. That didn't mean anything to shifters. They wanted sex, and when their partner was interested, they did it.

Telling herself she was being stupid didn't stop her from glancing towards the door again.

INTERVENTION

*C*oveney sipped his chocolate shake and took a bite of his pizza before turning to the play area and waving at the kids. The two eldest were reading on their tablets off to the side because they were too cool for inflatable castles today.

Rye had been right. It had been too long since they'd done this. Waiting around for enemies to turn up at their door had that effect.

Of course, it hadn't been why Rye had forced them all here, judging by the way everyone stared at him like they were trying to burn holes in his pizza.

He'd pretended not to let it get to him while he ate, because pizza was sacred. Now that he'd finished his last slice, he sighed, plopped his drink on the table, and said, "Alright, start the intervention, if you must."

He knew what they were about to say. *We don't know that girl. She's about to head to God knows where, for God knows how long, and you can't go. She isn't part of the pride.* And if Daunte had been talking behind his back, *you may be mistaken about her being your mate.*

That last part would piss him off more than the rest. The rest were valid concerns, but at each moment he was more certain that his educated guess had foundations. For example, right now, being five miles away from her was almost physically painful. And it had also started something, something deep, rooted in his tiger's instincts, bleeding through to him. A low, strange vibration that made him practically shake when he didn't watch himself.

He'd heard of that, too.

While he'd been close to her, so sure that he would get to touch her soon, fate had left him alone. Now that they'd forced some distance between them, now that they'd made him leave her with a single male - an annoyingly good-looking single male, at that - things had changed. He had mating urges. They were getting worse by the second. Harder. Stronger.

Let them speak and be done with it soon, so he could

return to her, where he belonged.

"Okay, so, don't get pissed," Rygan started, cautious. "But we just had to talk to you. For almost ten years, you've been a robot, a shadow of yourself. We've all seen it, even those of us who didn't know you before the mess with Lorren. Vivicia may joke and call you Robocop, but that's what you were, a damn robot. Frankly, it worried the shit out of us. All of us."

Nods all around. Coveney frowned. He'd seen their lingering glances, of course, especially Rye's. He'd just assumed they were disappointed in some way, not worried.

"I'm not the suicidal kind."

"No, but you weren't living either. Then, all of a sudden, you woke up from the funk. One day with a chick, *just one day*, and you're like a lovesick puppy. You talk. You smile. You joke. You're basically as crazy as Ace when someone gets the catnip out."

"I resemble that," the Alpha female commented with a sigh.

Coveney smiled. Ace really was embarrassing around catnip toys.

"See? Doing the smiling thing again. What I wanted to say, what we *all* wanted to say, is that we're not letting you throw that away out of duty."

He had to do his best to prevent himself from laughing. So, that's what they'd wanted to say? He shook his head.

Everyone glared at him, as if daring him to contradict them, except Daunte, who was too busy stealing some pizza from his mate's plate.

"And you?" he asked the Beta pair. "You've also come to preach?"

Daunte shrugged, absolutely shameless. "Nah. I was in when Rye said pizza. Plus, I would have punched that damn wolf if we'd stayed longer."

"You found the Scion woman yummy, I think his immortal sexiness is dreamy," Clari replied, slapping his hand away from her last slice. "Mine."

Coveney rolled his eyes, before getting up. "If that's all, you wouldn't mind if I head back ahead of you guys?"

"Wait, we're not done discussing..."

"What? Me letting my fated mate get away?" he lifted a brow as half of the table gaped at him. "I owe you guys, I really do. But that was never going to happen. Now, I need to get back to her. Especially given the fact that she's with... his immortal sexiness."

He grimaced, guessing the jerk would probably love the appellation.

"Coveney," Rye called him back. "She might really need to leave."

He nodded stiffly.

"If... when you go, know that there's always a place for you back with us. Both of you."

He smirked and said, "Hadn't doubted it," before shifting and running back towards Lakesides at full speed.

It was the first time he'd let his tiger out since the previous day, which seemed like a million years ago. The animal had always been focused and powerful, but he didn't think he'd ever run at that speed; he barely touched the ground, pushing his massive frame forward harder, faster, each time he leaped. At long last, he was in front of the pride house. He didn't bother shifting back, bumping his head on the front door until someone came to open it. The wolf girl. Vivicia, Coveney thought, but his tiger ignored her and kept on going until he finally found her.

Mate.

He pushed his head onto her lap and tilted it; she immediately took the hint and ran her fingers through his white fur, making him groan in pleasure.

Coveney hadn't lied; he didn't touch people, not even his pride mates, and his tiger was even worse. Right now, he couldn't comprehend what he'd had against it. His large paws covered her arms, making sure to keep her in place because if she stopped scratching him, he might just die.

Catnip indeed. Rye had nailed it.

"Hey, Coveney," she said, smiling down at him like he was the best thing she'd ever seen.

A second ago, the tiger had been so fond of her touch he was all but ready to overthrow his human self and become feral if it meant he could just carry on being touched by their mate. But when she said his name he immediately shifted, needing to be able to talk to her, too. Plus, the tiger readily admitted that he needed hands to remove all those bothersome clothes she wore over her soft skin. His claws wouldn't do the trick.

Shifting back faster than he ever had in the past, Coveney gathered her in his arms, and started to walk away, ignoring everyone in the room.

"What are you- where are you taking me..."

"Everywhere. I'll take you everywhere."

He completely ignored Knox, who sighed dramatically, telling Vivicia, "Am I the only one who may just vomit?"

MATES

*I*n all his naked glory, sporting an erection that should have alarmed her, the heathen carried her all the way back to the room where he'd nursed her the previous night, and dropped her on his bed.

"Didn't we clarify that I'm not some goddamned prize, Coveney Walker?"

"Did we?" he replied, and she had a perfect answer that would have indeed shown him his place, but, as he happened to capture her lips just then, she was too busy panting and melting under him to formulate a sound.

Okay, so she moaned, but that didn't count.

The man was completely naked and hovering over her on a large bed that smelled like him; Ava's insides melted, and her hips curved upward, needing to touch him.

"So beautiful," he whispered, his knuckles tracing her face, pushing her hair away. He opened his fist and let his hands slide over her bare arms. That was supposed to be innocent, right? So why did it feel like her clit was on fire?

Coveney chuckled. "You really don't believe it."

"Aria, my sister, she was the..."

"I didn't know Aria. I just know hundreds of women, and none of them have captivated me nearly as much as you."

Bedroom talk was always sweet, she told herself. This was normal. Her heart had no reason to beat at five thousand miles an hour, yet it went and did just that anyway.

"You know why, Ava? No, I expect you don't."

She didn't know anything at all right now, given the fact that his hand had reached her waist and he was pushing her borrowed tank top up, one excruciatingly slow second at a time.

For Christ's sake, she'd had guys go down on her, she shouldn't be panting like a crazy person because he was touching her damn tummy.

Impatient, needing him to give more, she reached between them, grabbed his cock, and started pumping it.

Coveney groaned, before chuckling. "You want this over with. You want me to shut up and fuck you so we don't have to talk about this. Funny, Ava. I didn't take you for a coward."

"I've had the birds and bees conversation with my momma, handsome. I need you."

"And I you. I just was going to make it clear that when I stop holding myself back in a minute, I'm going to bite or scratch you." His head dropped to her neck. He licked it before dropping feather-light kisses on it, as his frame dropped onto hers, his heavy cock grinding against her pants, and she threw her head back. Shit. Her clothes needed to go.

Wait, had he just said *bite*?

"Where do eagles mark each other, *mate*?" he whispered against her ear, and everything around them ceased to exist.

Mate.

Mate.

Mate.

Her animal, who'd remained watchful and careful

until now, who hadn't known what to make of him, cried out inside her. *Mate,* she said. The eagle felt as stupid as Ava, because they both should have seen it. Now, they did.

She wasn't in charge of her change this time; the eagle acted all on her own, morphing her hand, and running her talon from the small of his back to his shoulders, hard, deep, and slow.

Coveney winced, but stayed still until she was done. Then, he chuckled.

"I guess that answers that question."

"Sorry, I don't know what came over her, she just..."

"Don't you dare apologize." Then, he said it again. "Mate."

Fuck. He was hers.

If she hadn't marked him quite as brutally, brusquely, and without warning, they might have been more civilized about it. But, as things were, Ava opened her jeans and glided them down her legs. She lifted her knees to get them past her thighs, but, without giving her a second to do it, Coveney grabbed her arms, pinned them above her head, and plunged balls deep inside her in one hard thrust.

She yelled out in pleasure and surprise. Sitting up, Coveney angled himself to hit the deepest point inside her and thrust in again, and again, and again, so fast it was all a blur of sensations. Every single muscle inside her was tenser than ever when he clawed at her top, ripping it to shreds, before descending on her breast.

He bit her hard, drawing blood as she yelled out, her pussy contracting around him as he exploded inside her.

They were entirely still and silent for an instant. Her bird cooed happily, and Coveney's eyes flashed light blue, like his tiger's.

Mate.

She felt it in her heart, beating alongside his. In her blood and her bones. He was hers, and she was his.

Laughing softly, he finally finished helping her out of her pants, before kissing her ankles, and placing each of them on one of his shoulders, spreading her legs.

"I sincerely hope you're well-rested, Ava mine," he purred as his thumb pressed on her clit, the shallow movement of his hips reawakening every part of her. "This may just last a little while."

SUCKER PUNCH

*A*fter taking his mate all night, Coveney should have had a hard time moving. The first thing he saw when he woke up, though, was his mark, right on her breast, and he just had to kiss it.

There was a long, elegant symbol drawn on her skin now, like a perfectly healed tattoo, which had appeared overnight. It was the sexiest thing he'd ever seen, proving that they had been shaped by nature, destined to belong to each other. He wished he had a mirror to see his on his back where she'd claimed him.

She moaned, so he then had to kiss her lips, too. And, somehow, he found his dick pushing inside her wet folds from the side. Turned out, he could move just fine.

He could also move fine in the shower.

What he did have a hard time doing, though, was talking. But that conversation couldn't wait.

"So, how did Knox's idea go?"

The words practically strangled him on the way out. He saw it now, there was never any choice. He would have to go with her when she left, and if she chose to stay away, there was nothing he could do about it.

"Surprisingly well, so far. Most of the Alphas agreed to talk to me. When your tiger barged in yesterday, we were actually arguing about whether it could be done via Skype. Rain's idea. I think it would probably suit everyone - there are *a lot* of flocks of eagles, and it might take months to manage to get us all in one place. But a group conversation online - that could be done tomorrow."

He lifted a brow, incredulous. "So, you wouldn't need to go anywhere?"

"Well, if they are going to attack Dale for me, I probably *should* be there, I think. But, let's face it, even if each Alpha only brings two people with them, that's practically two hundred eagles. The Enforcers who rose against my family? There are only a dozen of them. The Dale flock doesn't even have fifty members. With their backing, it's just a formality."

"And then what?"

She frowned.

"It's you and me, now. I need to know what you want. If you'd like to go back to Dale..."

"I already said I didn't. I meant it."

He thought she had at the time. "There're an awful lot of people who seem to see you as their Alpha."

Coveney was strong, powerful, loyal, and smart, but he was no Alpha. Not a born Alpha, in any case.

Ava...

When he'd first seen her, she'd taken an arrow to save what she, on some basic level, must have understood was hers. Before, unbeknownst to him, she'd intervened to help his entire pride. She was shy, and her confidence level needed a boost, but those issues didn't cloud the rest. He saw it plainly - just like Aisling, she was born to rule.

He intended to show her, and tell her everything she was until she saw it, too. But it might mean they'd have to leave the pride he loved for good.

She just snorted.

"You think I want power."

Not really; she didn't want it. That didn't mean that

it didn't belong to her.

"Listen to me. My parents begged me to start diplomatic trips. That means going all over the world to show my face and remind the other flocks that the Dales are stronger than them. I tagged along when I was a child, and I freaking *hated* it. It's not that I can't do it. I genuinely can't stand it. Will I get them to help today? Yes. Totally. Because, if I don't, those Enforcers will carry on sending hunters after me and my brother. But once that's done, I'm walking away."

He pulled her to him and buried his head in her hair, inhaling her scent as she added, "I may have come to this particular pride because I thought you could help, but I wanted to stay from the start. I still do. It's peaceful here. I love the lake, and the townsfolk who somehow seem fine with you. I like the kids and your weird, intense Alphas. And, more to the point, this is my mate's pride. This is where you belong. So, of course we're staying here."

He breathed out, all the while thinking he was utterly fucked. Someday, soon, he was going to love her so damn much he wouldn't ever be able to live without her.

If he was entirely honest, although it made zero sense, given the fact that they'd met one day ago, he probably already did. Fate had sucker punched him in the teeth and there was nothing he could do.

FLYING

*A*va had never felt more awkward. There were a few dozen chat windows open, and glancing through them, she saw large, hard men and women flanked by equally impressive Betas and Enforcers. In her human form, she was small for an eagle.

But, instead of fidgeting like she wanted to do, she smiled.

She greeted everyone, effortlessly translating her statement into the language of those who addressed her. This was... easy. Familiar. Just like assisting her brother as he negotiated a deal, although he wasn't there to do part of the talking. It didn't matter. She'd seen it done many times, enough to know when she needed to summon her inner Richard and reply sternly, or when she needed to be herself, laughing it off and throwing in a joke to relax everyone.

Her biggest fear had been them balking at the fact that she was flanked by a feline shifter who she introduced as her mate, and it did annoy them. Eagles didn't make alliances, because their loyalty was entirely to the Flavia Dale. She guessed they'd see her as a hypocrite for mating outside of her own kind.

"So, what then? Let's say we somehow storm Dale, an impenetrable magical fortress, and kill all your enemies. Are you going to return to it and reign over us with your *cat*?" said a Russian Alpha.

Coveney kept his snarl in check. She didn't.

"With all due respect, Ryder, insult my mate to my face one more time and I'll pay you a visit."

The words were out of her mouth before she considered how stupid they would seem to a powerful Alpha. But instead of laughing in her face, like she thought he might, he stiffened and scratched his head.

It was then that it hit her. They weren't seeing an awkward five-foot-two girl right now. They looked at her and saw what she wanted them to see. The person she summoned when she needed courage: her eagle. The female was faster than Rupert, larger than Aria, and deadlier than Richard.

Through the embedded video screen reflecting her image, she saw her eyes turn fiery, losing their violet tint. She blinked, getting it under control, before smiling pleasantly.

Ah, hell. Their concern wasn't unwarranted.

"I have no intention of returning to Dale, and no intention of ruling any of you. It's past time our kind entered the twenty-first century, don't you think? You're capable Alphas. I don't call you to do my bidding now because you owe it to my family. I'm asking for your help. What I offer in return is *my* loyalty. I also offer Dale."

That got their attention. Not every eagle out there saw Dale, they'd had to be formally invited, but they'd all heard of it, no doubt.

"If you would assist me against them, I propose to make Dale, the birth place of our kind, a sanctuary where any eagle, and their friends, would be welcome, at any time. To my knowledge, there're around five thousand of us spread out across the world. Dale can accommodate that many people at any given time."

As the city wasn't quite hers to give that casually, she added, "Most of the current inhabitants of Dale, my old flock, are innocent of any wrongdoing, and I won't see them punished unless they take arms against us. They're to carry on however they wish, electing a leader of their own after we're gone."

She'd purposefully left the matter of the First lines alone, but they'd known the Alphas would bring it up, of course.

"But what about what they say?"

"Are the legends a lie?"

Ava shrugged. "I don't know, probably. It does sound like a children's tale, wouldn't you say? I'm simply asking for help because I don't want to die. My other solution would be asking my Alpha for his protection. That means the Wyverns and their allies - felines, wolves, bears, witches - descending on Dale."

It was hard to prevent herself from smiling. Yeah, she'd expected their reaction alright. "Dale belongs to *us!*"

"Eagles resolve our issues amongst ourselves!"

"Over my dead body."

Truth was, she would never have asked Rye and Ace to fight in Dale because they would all have died trying, unless they brought a few Scions along.

If they saw felines in their city, *every* eagle would attack, not just the traitors. Her stomach churned at the very thought of that mess. For all their raw power, felines wouldn't have a chance.

Most Alphas muttered with their seconds, and she saw dozens of them nod.

"Okay, so what's the plan?"

She winced, knowing Coveney was going to freak out. Big time.

~

"*I* should purchase a private jet. Awfully convenient," Knox remarked, looking out the small plane's window.

Ava disagreed. In actual fact, if she never got into a flying metal tube ever again, it would be soon enough. She would have snorted if she wasn't too busy attempting not to throw up, her head stuck between her legs as she breathed fast.

The only other person who seemed to realize that planes were evil was the Wyvern Alpha's son, who had cried at the top of his lungs from the moment they'd taken off.

"There, there," Ace cooed, rocking him in her arms.

The baby wasn't having any of it.

"May I?"

Rye, Coveney, and Jas, the short-haired, kick-ass Wyvern female she'd just met for the first time, as she'd been patrolling during the entire duration of her stay, stared at the First Wolf like he'd lost his goddamned mind. They gasped in unison when their Alpha female got up and just handed him her kid. Ava would have laughed, but, well, that probably meant vomiting on her shoes. And she liked her shoes.

Ace rolled her eyes at her mate.

"He isn't going to eat him," she said. Rye seemed to think that was debatable.

But it turned out, the wolf wasn't a baby eater as much as a baby whisperer. After two minutes of baby talk, at most, the child was done yelling.

"There's a good boy," the wolf praised him, tickling his tummy.

Little Zack shifted in the wolf's arms, and Knox stared in wonder.

"Kitten," he breathed, tightening his grasp like he half expected the kid to try to break free.

But, instead, it extended its little paws and stretched.

The wolf growled low. "I need one of these."

Most of the pride laughed; the child was pretty damn hard to resist.

Ava might have found it sweet if she didn't recall their previous conversation. Knox obviously liked babies, and wanted one, too, but he had none of his own.

Had he tried modern medicine? Was there some sort of workaround? He'd been born somehow, the process couldn't be that hard to replicate.

A smartly-dressed flight attendant wearing red and gold walked back in. "If you could please return to your seats and fasten your seatbelts, we're about to start landing. It's seven o'clock, and the temperature currently is seventy-four degrees in Rome. Rome is nine hours ahead of California; may I recommend you attempt to go to bed in good time this evening in order to minimize..."

The woman carried on going on about trivial things as the metal tube tilted towards the ground and started vibrating like someone was shaking it.

Typical. She was going to die flying.

ROME

$\mathcal{C}$oveney was a basic, overly excited American tourist and he wasn't even sorry about it.

"Look at this!" he exclaimed, dragging Ava from one ruin to the next, and she played along.

He winced, recalling she was born here - or anyway, some hidden valley not too far from here. "Sorry if I'm boring you."

She beamed. "Not at all. I actually haven't often come to Rome. I find the Forum fascinating. See there? These little holes on the old part of the building, the ones that weren't renovated and reinforced? That's an indication that the walls were covered with marble, a while back. They fitted it in that way.

Sometimes, you can still see some stone stuck in there."

"How about these bigger ones?"

He listened to her explain how the large blocks of stone piled up to build the impressive monument and were perfectly aligned, which was exceptional for a structure that old. They'd managed that by putting holes in the middle of each block, and fitting in a bar; that way, they could add the next block like a piece of Lego.

"They filled those holes with metal - bronze, mainly - and that was precious, so these holes were made to get to it after the Catholics came into power and started stripping down reminders of the old faith."

He wasn't the only one listening in, and a British tourist asked her a couple of questions, evidently taking her for a tour guide.

Coveney smiled a little sadly. How she fit in, in this ancient, beautiful, foreign city.

"You're having fun," she noticed, and he shrugged casually.

"First time abroad. It's definitely different than learning about all this on TV. Besides, might as well distract myself from thinking about this insane plan of yours."

That last part was grumbled, communicating his lack of enthusiasm. But he'd caved, for various reasons. Firstly, the damn plan made an awful lot of sense, and he would have nodded along, quite happy to execute it, if it had involved just about anyone else. Secondly, and he admitted it as begrudgingly as any dominant male might, his female was wearing the trousers. Now that she'd shed a lot of her shyness, it was apparent to him that she out-dominated him. If he had a dominance level similar to his Alpha, or his Beta, for that matter, it would have been an issue, but Coveney found that he didn't care much. And, lastly, if she pouted and said please, there was nothing, absolutely nothing, he wouldn't give her. He was putty in her damn little hands. And she knew it.

"So, what next?"

"Next, you need to do something no one stepping in Italy should ever forgo," she said quite seriously.

He lifted a brow as he followed her.

Ten minutes later, he was moaning in pleasure.

"What the hell is this?"

She shrugged. "Ice cream."

He gave her a look. Yeah, right. He'd had ice cream before. This didn't qualify. Ice cream was refreshing and tasty; it wasn't supposed to make him feel like he'd grown a set of wings of his own and tasted the food of the gods.

"Come again? Why the hell don't you guys export that shit?"

She grinned. "Maybe it just tastes different when you eat it here."

That made an awful lot of sense. He bobbed his head, repeating a word that had often been on his mind since he'd met her. "Witchcraft."

He couldn't come up with another explanation.

As the day drew on, somewhere between the Coliseum and the Pantheon, he felt her grow stiff. It wasn't just that he saw her shoulders tense and smelled a difference in her; he felt it to his bones. His mate's worry transferred to him.

He wanted to ask, but he knew he couldn't.

Are they here? Are they watching?

Ava had said the second she'd return to Italy, the eagles of Dale would know it, and would go after her. Something about their ward warning of the master's return. It had probably been set in place so her folks could get ready to greet their Alphas after they came back from a trip. Who knew?

What mattered was that now her enemies were going to come after her.

Which would have been all well and good, if she wasn't expecting him to let them take her.

"They won't want to spill blood in Rome. Firstly, it makes more sense to abduct me and deal with me on their own turf than to potentially have to fight whatever ally I bring with me. Secondly, if I'm close to home, they won't be able to resist bringing me back to Dale, and parading me in front of everyone as their captive. They were quite dramatic with my parents and siblings," she'd grimaced with distaste.

How that was supposed to convince him to let them take her, he didn't know.

"Right. So, we let a merry band of psychopathic traitors take you where they can hurt you. Let's say, for the sake of argument, that this isn't the very definition of insanity. Then what?"

She smirked.

"Then, we crush them all."

*H*e'd only caved after listening to every single detail, and had her answer all his theories, all of his questions. The damn woman had eliminated every logical concern he'd voiced. Still, it didn't mean that he liked what he had to do.

"Just heading to the toilet, beautiful," he said, kissing her forehead one last time.

He looked into her violet eyes and held her gaze one beat too long for it to seem casual, but he couldn't say the words at the tip of his tongue. Stay safe. Come back to me.

So, instead, he simply told her, "I love you."

Her jaw dropped, and he simply winked before turning his back and heading away from her. He'd never done a harder thing in his entire existence.

HOME

*A*va resisted, kicking and screaming when they came at her. Recalling just what they'd done to her brother and sister when they'd gotten their hands on them, it was hard to allow them to take her. Very, very hard. The best she could do was hope that they'd planned to wait for them to get to Dale before starting her humiliation and torture.

One of the men managed to get his hand around her mouth and nose. An unpleasant stench filled her nostrils and she almost immediately started to lose focus, slowly blacking out.

How predictable they were. Still, she was pretty glad she'd been right, given that the alternative had been them just breaking her neck and getting it over with.

But she knew Roberto, Max, Antonio, Neri, and she

most definitely knew Angela. Others had joined them, but as the old Enforcers, they were the main force behind the treason. They wouldn't have been able to resist making a show of it, demonstrating that she wasn't better than them.

Two of them were Richard's age, the others, older, and she'd known them all her life. She couldn't recall ever saying one unkind thing to them, or acting like a superior brat, for that matter. That wasn't her personality.

Aria had been a little on the arrogant side, perhaps. Rupert, too, although his vanity was mainly about his abilities; he'd loved to spar with the Enforcers, knowing he'd win.

Still, none of that mattered. Her time away from Dale had taught her that what she'd considered normal for so long, what her family had, really wasn't natural.

Most other kinds of shifters had ruling packs, prides, and flocks, like wolves and felines, but those groups left the rest of their peers to do what they wanted on an ongoing basis; they only interfered when there was a true need for it. The Flavians hadn't overseen the rest of the flocks; they'd ruled. And their monarchy had been despotic. Fair, just, caring, she'd liked to think, but still absolute.

It had only been a matter of time before someone rebelled, and, honestly, Ava even saw it as a necessary thing. As she'd said to the other Alphas, it *was* the twenty-first century, and even vampires had realized that no one liked to be ruled.

They hadn't only desired to overthrow them, though. They wanted to eradicate them, not realizing that it would really mean their own doom. They'd done what they'd seen as necessary.

Well, not just that. They'd enjoyed killing her family and they'd taken pleasure in hurting her siblings.

Ava didn't have a choice.

*T*he drug they'd used only knocked her out for an hour, but she had the sense to control her breathing, and pretend sleep, because while her consciousness came back quickly, she didn't immediately regain control of her body.

If they'd paid attention, the shifters driving her would have felt the difference, but they were too giddy and victorious to care.

Although her eyes were blindfolded, and closed underneath, she felt it the second she passed the immaterial barrier keeping the rest of the world away from Dale. Some of her weariness disappeared, and, in her heart, despite everything that had happened here, she knew she was home.

"Did Max get everyone to the forum?" she heard Neri ask.

"No, just us. He said he wanted to make sure the bitch was broken before he showed her to the flock. You never know, they might try to free her or something. Why they all seem to care so much about her, I'll never know."

"She wasn't the worst of them," Roberto admitted reluctantly. "I would have preferred getting my talons on her brother."

She managed to keep her gasp quiet. So Richard *was* alive. She hadn't let herself think about it too much; if she didn't know, she wasn't one hundred percent sure he was gone.

She smelled a familiar fragrance, indicating they'd reached the far edge of the city, where the Bianchi family made the best wines and cheese; they were close. Tentatively, she attempted to move a finger, and smirked when it worked.

Then, she waited.

If she wasn't mistaken, she had three abductors. They parked the van and walked out towards the back to grab her, chatting casually along the way.

"What do you think Max will do to her, then?"

"Oh, I don't know, but he's going to make a point - if we make it dirty and let the word spread, no doubt her brother will rush here to defend her honor. Then, we can get them all."

Great plan, actually. Just not as good as hers.

"What if..." Neri cleared his throat. "I know they showed us proof that they weren't even around when they said they were, that they aren't related to the Flavia, but what if they were wrong? You know. Killing them both... that could mean our own end."

"Don't you worry about that. Max doesn't plan on risking it. Richard, we'll kill, but we're keeping the bitch alive, just in..."

He'd opened the door, the idiot. Her eagle burst out of her skin so fast the chains binding her hands and feet were torn to shreds, along with her clothes. Although the animal would have loved to stay and scratch their eyes out, she just bulldozed her way through the three shifters. Her absolute priority was in line with Ava's.

They needed Coveney here.

And, alright, a few other allies wouldn't hurt, but if they didn't succeed, they'd never see him again. Which wasn't an option.

She heard a high-pitched call, too close to ignore, but, against her instincts to turn and fight whoever was coming at her, she flew straight towards the very place where they'd wanted her.

She was lucky they had been fed some nonsense that made them disregard everything her family had said. Otherwise, they might never have brought her to Dale. Otherwise, they definitely wouldn't have planned to take her to the forum, a long open roofed hall with high columns at each side, each of which was adorned with statues. Unlike the rest of what may have been done back in the day, it wasn't effigies of gods; they were symbols of nature - trees, leaves, fire, air, earth. Some showed stars, too.

Never slowing to soften her landing, she crashed onto the floor, and begged her eagle to let her shift back immediately. The bird relented instantly, giving her back her limbs, and more importantly, her vocal cords.

There, right in the middle of the place where their initial protection spell had been cast, she said one simple word.

"Aperire."

Good thing she was proficient in Latin, too.

As they were bid by their rightful owner, every ward clouding Dale from the eyes of the world opened.

HELPLESS DAMSEL

So, that was an insight into what insanity might be like. Coveney stared into the void, the empty road ahead, where the rest of them had been waiting.

The eagles had been reluctant to let them – Coveney, Ace, Rye and Knox – tag along on their little rescue mission, but his Alphas hadn't budged. Ava was part of their prides, and they had no intention of being kept out of the action. They'd relented. Good thing, too: nothing could have kept Coveney away from Ava.

The eagles that had visited Dale in the past swore it was there. All he saw was a bunch of strangers, along with his Alphas and Knox, all waiting on the side of the road. Jas had stayed at their hotel with Zack.

The only thing that kept him from entirely losing his mind was that, somehow, he *felt* her.

"How does this thing work? According to Google Maps, there's nothing here."

"It wouldn't be much of a magical ward if it showed up on Maps," Knox remarked.

Still, he didn't know it was possible to so completely cloak anything, let alone an entire city.

"Witches were a little more 'hard rock' back in the day," the wolf explained. "Virgin sacrifice, firstborns, orgies. All that stuff makes for stronger magic than what they do now."

"So when," he wasn't saying if, "she pulls the wards down, it's going to appear on Maps. Can she put them back up?"

Knox shook his head. "No living coven I know of can manage that. We're going to watch regulars freak out that there's a whole city out there that they didn't know a thing about. And talk about real estate value."

An eagle chuckled. "Yeah, let them try to take it from us."

"If I heard it right, the Flavian kept records old enough to make any historian hard. There's no way..."

Knox stopped talking because all of a sudden, Dale was there, right in front of his eyes.

If no one had told him the place was called Dale, Coveney might have gone with the Garden of Eden, or maybe Olympus. Picturesque didn't begin to cover it. There was a valley covered with fields, some green, some golden, smelling of freshly cut hay. He saw sunflowers, poppies, grapes; a few horses ran freely at the bottom of a large hill. Rows of cypress trees led to a white city; each flat-roofed, elegant house seemed fit for a king. Right at the peak, there was a palace. They were too far away, so Coveney didn't see its fountains, its obsidian and gold halls, its statues by the world's most acclaimed artists over the ages. Still, he said, "Well, fuck me," right before he shifted, and started running towards his mate.

*T*he eagles made it first, obviously. He knew they would. What he hadn't expected was that none of them would have had any work left by this point.

It wasn't like the rebels had all of a sudden decided to lay down their arms and surrender, either. By the looks of it, they'd at least attempted to fight their way out of it.

When he made it, Ava was standing naked in the

middle of the forum, holding a stranger hard in her little arms. He was in an equal state of undress and bloodiness. It pissed Coveney off for all of two seconds, before he saw the tall, muscular shifter's violet eyes.

Richard. That was her brother.

He forced himself to stay back, to let her have her moment.

There were various body parts at their feet, bird and human.

"You do know some of your avian friends came from China for this, right?" Knox mused out loud.

He didn't seem to mind being thoroughly ignored.

The siblings finally turned to them, both grinning from ear to ear. The moment they did, Coveney let his animal pounce and rub himself all over her legs to make sure she was really there, really in one place.

"Richard, this is my mate, Coveney."

He narrowed his eyes, zeroing in on the white tiger.

"A cat."

Coveney roared in response. Would it *kill* them all to say 'tiger' instead?

"Oh, no, don't you start being a pain, brother. Maybe

if you'd looked at other breeds of shifters, you might have found your own mate."

Richard snorted.

"See this?" he pointed to the bodies. "Mess up and you'll *wish* I'd just dismembered you."

"Threaten him and you'll just *wish* I didn't have incriminating pictures of you," his mate defended him as he shifted back.

His tiger had needed reassurance, but so did he. Pulling her towards him, burying his head in her hair and inhaling all her sweetness, he finally breathed easily.

"What happened?"

"Everything went as planned."

She was lying. He could tell.

"Ava..."

"She was reckless," Richard filled in. "Hurt herself on her way down and found herself surrounded by enemies, with a bad arm. Which was lucky for them, or it wouldn't have been a challenge. She'd managed to blind that one," he waved towards a corpse, "and bite that one's finger off when I made it. Gave her a second to shift. Then, well," he winced, then shrugged. "They started it."

Fuck. He wanted to ask how whatever they'd done had resulted in so many bits and pieces of people, but thought better of it.

Rye couldn't help himself, though. "How the heck did you get a dozen full-grown eagles? I mean, they did take your flock."

Ava averted her eyes. Again, her brother had no issue spelling things out. "We lost, last time, because none of us thought to fight. Our parents were too shocked, our siblings were too freaked out. I flew out immediately to try to find Ava..."

"And I'd run," the woman filled in, darkly. "We lost because I was too cowardly to stay and fight."

It was more than that, though. In a few days, he'd seen a shift in her. He didn't know her as well as he wanted to – not yet – but he'd peeked at her insecurities, her belief that she wasn't worth as much as the rest of her siblings, when he'd first met her. Perhaps thanks to Knox, or to the Alpha eagles who'd chosen to follow her, that was gone now. And what was left was a powerful, determined, dominant leader.

Coveney smirked. Yeah. He was going to be the bottom for the rest of his days.

The Alphas she'd called to her aid were watching, visibly uneasy at what they'd witnessed.

"Sorry, I did genuinely think I needed help," she told them.

Her brother ruffled her hair, calling her an idiot.

"Still, you came, and I'll keep my word." She glanced towards Richard. "This place should belong to all of us. The whole history of the world, from the shifter point of view, is recorded in our library - I don't think anyone else has a full account like that."

"I beg to differ," Knox piped in.

Her brother nodded slowly. "Whatever you say. This place gives me the creeps anyway."

The Alphas didn't seem reassured. Finally, one spoke.

"This isn't normal. I've heard your family trained well, but it should have taken an entire flock to tear them apart like that. You... there's a reason why you guys were the head of our kind."

There was. Not one that she was willing to say out loud, though. She held the Alpha's gaze without saying a word, until he looked away.

"Dale can become a public place if you want," he said. "But the Ryder flock will still honor its pledge to your house."

Ava was taken aback, but instead of seeming all

awkward, like Coveney thought she might, she inclined her head at the same time as her brother, accepting it gracefully.

Each Alpha swore the same oath that day, as Ace and Rye carefully watched from a distance. Coveney stayed at Ava's side, feeling like a queen's consort. There were worse things. Especially since, while she may have the upper hand in practically every other aspect, there was still one place where he was on top.

"*P*lease!*" she yelled, shamelessly begging at the top of her voice.

He wasn't having any of it, keeping her knees wide open and suckling on her folds, making her tremble and try her best to move. With her hands tied to the head of their bed, and her legs pinned in place, she had her work cut out for her.

"Please what, beautiful?"

He smirked as she glared at him. Shrugging, he just carried on teasing her pussy, stopping each time the pace of her breathing got faster, each time she started to reach the edge.

"You're going to have to spell it out. It's not like I can guess what you want me to do, can I now?"

The woman cursed him in a bunch of languages he

didn't recognize; he was pretty sure he got the gist of it, though. It was killing her. She was just too polite and well-bred to talk dirty, which made it imperative that he had to hear her do it.

Plus, she totally deserved it for making him worry for hours.

Eventually, she caved, screaming, "Please let me fucking come!" and who was he to deny his mate?

Flipping her to her hands and knees, he entered her painfully slowly from behind, relishing the feeling of her around him.

Damn, that ass. One glance at it, and he was pounding like his life depended on it; for all he knew, it just might. She met his hips, taking him hard and fast. The sound of their breathing, and the slap of his legs and balls hitting her, surrounded them until they fell off the edge together.

"Coveney?"

"Mh?"

"You do know my brother's room's next door, right?"

He laughed nervously. "Ah, hell. At least my last night on earth was pleasant." She chuckled against his chest.

"Coveney?"

"Hm?"

"You know, that thing you said before, in Rome…"

Ah, shit. He knew she was going to bring it up eventually. He kissed her perky little nose and told her, "Don't worry. I'm aware it's completely insane to feel that way after… five days, was it? You don't have to say it back."

"I know I don't have to," Ava said. Then she left it at that. For so long he'd actually started breathing again when she added, "But I still love you, too."

EPILOGUE

MEANWHILE, CHRISTINE…

*H*anging up, Christine beamed at everyone, announcing, "They're all coming back. No one's hurt. They didn't even need to fight, so it's basically turned into an Italian holiday."

Vivicia, who'd stayed longer than she ever did to make sure they had enough fighters protecting the pride in Coveney, Ava, Ace and Rye's absence, rolled her eyes, muttering, "Typical."

Christine couldn't blame her. A few days in Rome would have been a lot of fun, but she never resented her position. It was an important one, although some people didn't think so. The pride understood it. Whenever she spent a few days away, they all treated her like a long-lost sister at her return.

They were a kick-ass, flamboyant, dominant bunch. She didn't feel the need to try to prove she was better than anyone. She didn't need to fight, either, although she could and would defend herself.

Christine was a submissive, and proud of it, too. Proud of loving and caring for her pridemates. She got up earlier than most to get their breakfast ready. She spent more time with the children than any of the others. Although she was twenty-eight, she was basically their mom. Except she got paid more than your average Manhattan executive.

She wasn't a maid. They had a cleaner coming in every other day and they actually alternated the cooking duties - most of them had their turn, although they generally begged Ian to do it more often than the others. The man was a damn gourmet chef.

Breakfast was her domain because she loved it. It was the one time they really felt like a big, boisterous family.

"Mama," Lola called.

She'd taken to calling all the females *Mama,* since she'd started spending time with other kids in Lakesides. Because they had mothers and she didn't understand why she didn't have one, no one minded, least of all Christine. Beaming at her, she held her up in her arms and asked, "What is it, Lola bear?"

"There's a doggy in the garden."

She turned, frowning. Dogs didn't generally get close to shifters, let alone wild cat shifters.

The garden was completely empty, but she carried on watching past it, towards the trees behind their walls. Her eyes flashed, and she held on to Lola a little tighter.

She wasn't a fanciful child, which made her words all the more alarming.

There were plenty of wolves in the world and some wanted to take Lola from them.

~

The wolf watched them curiously. His attention had been focused on the child, first, but now she'd caught his eye, the redheaded female holding her seemed positively mouth-wateringly fascinating.

Hunter should have left then. He'd promised himself he'd only catch a glance.

But his wolf and he both decided they weren't going anywhere just yet.

The End

Christine and Hunter's story is next in the Age of Night Series.

You may remember Hunter from Kitty Cat; he's the son of the Vergas Pack Alpha...

NOTE FROM MAY

I'm so glad I *finally* got to introduce Knox properly. I first mentioned him in Wordless, and he's briefly poked his nose here and there though this series, but it's the first time I actually described him!
My beta readers have all asked about him. Just a head's up: yes, he's getting his story. No, it's not planned right now. It's a 2018 project, mainly because it will be pretty long.
Follow me on Facebook for updates on things like that.

Now, the next book in this series is Cats and Dogs, Christine's story, but also look out for the spin offs.

The next one is Hunky Beast, a spin off Pretty Kitten, featuring Emily, the woman Daunte rescues.

The following one is the Loner's Mate... Richard's story!

Stay in tune for a few short excerpts of upcoming work.

REALM OF DARKNESS

UNEDITED EXCERPT

*S*he wasn't surprised. Why wasn't she surprised?

Tria was contemplating theories to answer that mystery, holding the door open, and Gray must have taken it as an invitation, because he walked past her, getting in the office.

"What is he..." Daphne started, but Tria tuned her cousin out, because the idiotic, suicidal stranger took a step towards her, getting right in her personal space, and bent down to hold his face so close to hers she could feel his breath on her shoulder.

Daphne could very well be screaming about a shark in a pink tutu, Tria wouldn't have given two fucks about it, right then.

"Brown," Mr. Suicidal said, pulling back. "You have brown eyes."

What the... Did he realize she could very well have beheaded him for taking her by surprise like that?

Probably not.

"Black, actually," she ~~replied~~ retorted. "What are you doing here? You know it takes special clearance to come to us, right?"

"I lead the First Squad."

He shrugged it off like it was nothing; it wasn't. The First Squad were some of the best this Agency had. They also were Agents who were there of their own volition; not flight risk, or potential enemies like so many others. Her eyes narrowed, and she attempted to see past the highly distracting facade. Was he some sort of spy? To test their loyalty to the Agency? She would have thought the possibility highly plausible if the director hadn't been so damn stupid and naive. But Andy really believed they were happy at the Agency.

He'd replaced his predecessor five years prior; he hadn't seen them before they'd learned to hide their feelings. He had their files, of course, but he'd dismissed their previous behavior as their excessive version of teenage rebellion.

Tria was the least problematic out of the three of them, and there was a simple reason for that. She was the only one who wasn't a prisoner.

*T*en years ago, her mother's parting words told her to get to the newly formed agency. "You aren't alone, Tria."

She hadn't known what she'd meant then, but she'd obeyed. It wasn't like she'd had many options, at fifteen, without any documents proving her identity.

The agents had greeted her like a goddamned messhia, because they'd just caught a kid they couldn't control - or kill, for that matter. Daphne, younger than her by two years, had been found shoplifting; she killed the two policemen who tried to arrest her, before running for it. The Agency sent their best after her, and when they found her, shit hit the fan. She killed over half of them before they managed to restrain her long enough to shoot her with a sedative; the kind they used on Elephants. It had worked for a few minutes.

Tria recalled it well; at first glance, she recognized her for what she was.

Jase might have had a similar story, if things had gone differently. Slightly older than Tria, he had a job bussing tables, keeping his head down, but some human kids were stupid enough to try to corner him. To his credit, he didn't actually kill any of them, although Tria doubted they'd regained their motor function by now.

It took them a while to confirm that they were actually related, but now they knew. It couldn't be a coincidence. Three of times, at the same time, in the same place? Their parents were playing some games. Again.

Being together calmed them down - on the surface level, at least. When they felt like exploding, they could just punch each other until it passed. But that didn't change what was brewing underneath.

Daphne was a prisoner. She could never leave the agency without authorization and supervision. Jase was under surveillance. While Tria was free, she knew the second she stepped out of line, she would be considered a level five threat, like her cousin.

The Agency would send their dogs on them. They'd send the First Squad.

So, fuck him and his perfect...everything. She knew where they stood. Hunter and prey.

"Regardless of your qualifications, you're not supposed to be here without a rea..."

She didn't finish that sentence, because he pulled a bronze box out of his pocket. Her eyes zeroed in on it.

Shiny.

The dick smirked knowingly. Damn, how had he guessed that this was her Achilles heel?

"Sorry, what was that?" he gloated, pulling the box high, out of her reach, when she moved to take it.

She pouted.

"I got it from a raid last week. No one upstairs knows what it is. I had to pull some strings to get it out of storage and get it back, you know."

She glared, managing not to stomp her foot.

"Gimme."

He laughed softly and lowered it. She snatched it quickly, before he changed his mind.

Tria's eyes focused on the detailed carvings outside of the wooden box, her fingers tracing the fine line of bronze incrusted. Frustrated, she pulled her glasses from her nose, placing them on her head. It was generally not an issue, but they prevented her from using about ninety percent of her abilities. Her eyes now zeroed in *beyond* the box, beyond what lay inside. In the immaterial dimension, it looked like a blazing amber rune.

"Byzantine. It's authentic, but not quite Roman."

Her cousin, who'd shamelessly eavesdropped through the entire exchange, didn't even pretend they weren't paying attention now; they came closer, both curious.

"Can I see?" Daphne asked eagerly.

Of course she would. The seal atop the box would make it of particular interest to her.

"Careful," Tria warned her, holding her gaze.

She didn't mean that she shouldn't drop it, or damage it, and they both knew it. Daphne had to be careful not to let go of her power in font of a potential enemy.

The blonde snorted, in a way that made Tria frown, wondering what she meant. Jase tapped his temple, gesturing to Tria's hair. That's when she realized her mistake.

Shit.

Ten years. It had been more than ten years, and she'd *never* slipped in front of a stranger. But she'd just removed half of her damn mask.

Feeling confused, ashamed, and angry, she pulled it back on top of her nose, and snatched the box back from Daphne's hands, before throwing it at Grayson, without looking at him. She couldn't bring herself to.

"It's not dangerous," she lied.

It wasn't - as long as it never returned to Daphne's hands. She walked away, returning to her favorite alcove, but after a beat, he called after her, "What do I tell the archivist?"

Whatever you want, she wanted to scream.

Jase took over, spearing her.

"Back in the day, Christianity was rising and those who believed in the old gods either hid it, or died martyrs. Some of those who hid it prayed to their chosen deities. This," he said, "is an offering to Zeus - or Jupiter. See the symbol, on top? That's an oak tree. Inside, there's something that was infinitely precious to its bearer - doesn't matter what. It is believed that gods feed of faith, so they'd find that sort of things particularly precious."

Jase's liquid blue eyes shone when he told Gray. "Guard it. You never know which legends are true."

Tria had to smile a little.

Grayson left without knowing that he'd just been ruthlessly mindfucked.

"You'd get in trouble if this gets out," Daphne told him. "But thank you."

Jason shrugged it off, returning to his Xbox.

Eventually, she told herself that it wasn't the end of the world. Her little slip was inconsequential. He might not even have been looking at her. Right?

She lifted her head from the book she'd pretended to read, and cleared her throat to get Daphne's attention.

"Tell me, was that guy..."

"Yep. He saw you."

Shit. So much for that.

She couldn't help it.

"And?"

Daphne was smiling like she was enjoying the situation *way* too much.

"You didn't look at him. I doubt he fell for it."

Killing a SWAT team, now he was done with Zombies, Jase asked, "Is it really that bad? You never actually told me what happens to mortals who look at you. Are we talking Medusa bad, or what?"

Tria groaned, as Daphne smirked.

"Drop it."

"But..."

"Just drop it."

*H*e's the rising star of the Paranormal Investigation Agency; she'd love to burn it to the ground.

*T*ria Winters plays the part of the loyal agent well, but she's nothing short of a prisoner. When the Agency is brutally attacked, she and her cousins should have taken their chance to run, but to her surprise, there are people she isn't quite willing to turn her back on.

*I*t's obvious to Gray that Tria and her family are trouble, but they're the only ones who could fight off those who wish to destroy the Agency. He needs to stay with them.

*E*ven though their plan may land them all in Hell.

THE KRINAR'S BANE

SCI-FI ROMANCE

*E*very day, Zarken wondered why he bothered. Sincerely. He could have sent an employee, an apprentice; anyone, really. They didn't need *him* on Earth.

You came to this planet because you were bored, a little voice reminded him.

Yes, he had. And instead, he was bored and annoyed now, because the planet hadn't retained his attention past the first hour of his stay.

Krinars didn't have an organized army as such, but when the Elders saw a threat, they liked to have it assessed and, if need be, managed. That was where he came in.

The events that had occurred at the beginning of the summer – the foolish resistance humans had organized against his kind – had been neutralized with ease, but the Elders still felt that getting him involved was the wisest course of action. Pointless as it was, humans *would* risk losing lives in order to regain control over their planet. Never mind that they had no clue what to do with it. They'd been well on their way to destroying it before its time, when they'd intervened. But they *would* fight against them, because it simply was in their nature. War. Violence. They loved it. Needed it. Having an enemy to fight made their short lives feel meaningful, perhaps.

Not that Krinars could blame them, all things considered. Firstly, they had been lead and manipulated by other Krinars, but Zarken also gave them the benefit of the doubt, because his race wasn't a stranger to violence. The main difference was that, unlike humans, Krinars were aware of their tendency, and had found ways to address it responsibly.

No Krinar would ever act like the three drunken buffoons, or the prey they were closing in on, for that matter. They planned to rape the girl, or frighten her, at the very least. The girl hadn't been resourceful enough to avoid putting herself in this situation. Zarken wasn't sure who was more idiotic.

"Yeah? Gonna do something about it? There's one of you, and three of us," the sweaty, pungent human observed.

Zarken *hadn't* planned to intervene, actually. He would simply have alerted some sort of employee around here, and let humans deal with the human matter. No doubt their kind had some sort of punishment in place for harassing, or intending to harm, their females.

But then, the man had to go and make it personal, issuing a challenge. And Zarken *was* extremely bored.

"You might want to bring a dozen of your kind, and it may end up being a fair fight," he replied, feeling the corner of his mouth curve up.

Although, he was lying. A dozen wouldn't have cut it. Not against most Krinars, certainly not against *him.*

Zarken minimized his computer before placing it in the back pocket of his surprisingly convenient Earthen attire, and turned to the small group of humans, taking a good look at them for the first time.

That's when he saw her. The others faded in the background, becoming quite irrelevant as he scrutinized her eagerly, hungrily.

Not a girl, then; a woman. Zarken felt a familiar, yet unexpected yearning buzz through him as he met her deep brown eyes, and watched her mouth pop open. Interesting.

Sex was one of the few things that managed to rid him of the boredom for a while, but it was rare that he found a female to his taste. It had been years since anyone had caught his interest. Yet the human had his attention now.

Which was bad. For him, for her, and certainly for the males who'd wanted to harm her. Because yes, Krinars acted in a civilized manner, in general, but under the layers of cultivated etiquette, and reasonable behavior, they were something else entirely. Hunters. Creatures who'd savagely killed to protect their territory. There was only so much that evolution could do to erase that.

The woman had brown hair, falling in soft waves around her face, long lashes and smoldering eyes, but it was her plump lips that had retained his attention. He knew just what he wanted to do with those lips, and the heavy breasts highlighted by the sweetheart neckline of her pink dress.

If he could pick one word to describe his entire race, it would have been territorial, and right then, he almost felt like the stranger staring at him with her pretty mouth open was part of his territory.

"You may want to close your eyes, doll," he told her pleasantly, appreciating the way her cheeks reddened deeper yet. "It's not going to be pretty."

"Wait," one of the humans stuttered, "You're one of..."

He didn't finish his sentence, as Zarken's hand was already wrapped around his throat.

"Sorry, we didn't know she was with..."

He didn't hear the rest of the sentence, as he'd thrown the man to the end of the corridor and heard his bones crack at the impact. He slowly approached another while smiling, as he saw the last coward flee. He seized the heathen's skull and effortlessly pushed him down, forcing him on his knees.

"You can't kill him," his woman said, not sounding quite certain.

And she was right to doubt it; of course, he could. His kind weren't subject to human laws.

"Or anyway, you shouldn't," she amended. "I'm sure they've all learned their lesson."

Zarken turned to her, and instantly forgot what he'd been about to say, as the depth of her eyes hit him full force.

He narrowed his eyes.

"Do I look like a teacher, doll?"

"Do I look like a doll, Krinar?" she shot back, crossing her arms over her chest, which only served to make her delightful breasts pop up out of the tight, lacy top of her dress a little more.

He approved.

"Yes," he replied, baring his teeth. "Yes, you do."

And he had every intention of playing with his doll.

"They'll all live." Even the one he'd launched had got to his feet and scampered away. Under different circumstances, he might have chased him, and finished the job, but his attention was otherwise engaged. "As per your wishes."

Zarken moved at an excruciating pace, doing his best to appear non-threatening to the woman whose pulse quickened as her lips and cheeks darkened. He stopped two feet away from her, reluctant to crowd her space the way her would-be assailants just had. Perfectly familiar with human customs, after studying her kind for the last month, he extended his hand. When she placed hers in his palm, a sudden and entirely unexpected charge coursed through his body, shooting straight to his loins.

He'd known they had chemistry at first sight, but he hadn't expected that reaction from the most innocent touch.

How fascinating.

He lifted her hand up to his lips, and dropped a brief

kiss on the back of her palm, smirking as he saw, smelled, and felt her arousal. Despite a healthy dose of fear, the woman wanted him. Normally, some of his interested dwindled when he realized he wouldn't need to work for it, but to his surprise, he found himself pleased.

"May I, sweetest doll?"

She took an intake of breath without saying a word. She didn't need to. Zarken closed the space between them, lodging his leg between her thighs and pushing it to the apex, inciting a deep moan from her perfect mouth.

"So gorgeous," he whispered against her ear, taking his time to scent the aroma of her naked neck, before dropping his lips to its nape, while caressing her lower folds.

Without any volition, he found himself pushing his hardened cock against her stomach, letting her feel it through their layers of clothing. She moaned in response.

"I, I..." she stammered when his lips got an inch away from hers.

"Yes?"

His free hand ran down her arm, her leg, and played with the hem of her skirt, before sliding underneath the material, touching her naked skin. His cock twitched as he felt a flimsy, soft piece of fabric and pushed it aside.

"We're... in a club, in public..."

"Have you ever come in public, doll?"

She would.

His fingers got to her wet, glistening center just as he pressed his lips to hers and devoured her moans.

Her pussy was so slick, hot, and wet. He buried a finger deep inside, and explored each corner, circling her clit with his thumb and fucking her mouth with his tongue.

She panted, moving her hips against him, feeling her release ever so close.

There. There it was. Finally, at long last, her muscles relaxed and she covered his hand with her cum.

Chuckling, he removed his hand.

"Zarken," he introduced himself, and she blinked in blissful, post-orgasmic confusion. "That would be my name."

"Oh," she breathed. "I'm- er, oh God, I didn't even know your name and we just, I just..." she breathed out hard, and tried again. "Eva. I'm called Eva."

Humans also had a surname, and Zarken almost asked for hers, before thinking better of it. Why did it matter? He now knew what to call her while he pulled her hair and pounded her from behind tonight - beyond that, she was of no relevance whatsoever.

If there was one thing he was certain of, it was that he'd be bored before morning.

*P*eople say Eva's a little ditzy, when they want to be nice. Truth is, she's a magnet for trouble and she wouldn't know what caution looks like if she bumped into it.

But even she knows the delicious hunk she meets at the club is dangerous; he might have saved her once, but he could as easily destroy her and no one could do a thing about it. His kind is above reproach, above the laws, above humanity.

She should stay away.

She won't.

*A*fter thousands upon thousands of years, seeing empires rise and fall, Zarken is indifferent to everything, and entirely focused on his work.

Until her.

THE BIG BAD OFFICE WOLF

*A*fter the night of her life with a dirty, sexy stranger who's supposed to live a world and a half away from her, Tori is feeling pretty damn smug - until she finds him in the office next door.

Bryant is a menace, making every woman in the entire building lose focus, but she never thought he would actually go after her assistant.

Determined to save the poor girl from his clutches, she confronts him, and finds herself thrust in a world she never knew existed.

*B*ryant should stay away from the sweet little prim and proper thing wrapped in designer suits, but he's had a taste and he can't seem to forget it. He knows there's no way he can even pretend to be satisfied with a vanilla relationship. Good thing that when the clothes and the attitude come off, Tori might very well be a sub. All he needs is to lead her down the rabbit hole...

*D*isclaimer: *The big bad office wolf is a very steamy romance, more so than most of my books. As the description suggests, it also includes some BDSM element. Spare panties recommended.*

THE
BIG BAD
OFFICE WOLF
MAY SAGE
USA TODAY BESTSELLING AUTHOR

Printed in Great Britain
by Amazon